Choose Your Weapon . . .

The prisoner lashed out with his knife blade, swinging and slashing crazily. It must have been the way he attacked those men in the saloon. Longarm did not want to wind up the same way—lying on the saloon floor. Not only did he not want to, he had no intention of it.

He sidestepped another swing of the knife blade and went for his Colt.

The sound of the big .45's muzzle blast filled the small jail building and momentarily destroyed Longarm's hearing.

A lead slug driven by forty grains of black powder struck the farmer in the brisket and knocked him to his knees.

The man looked up at Longarm. His mouth formed a wide O but no sound came out.

He looked down at the knife he still held in his right hand. Then he toppled forward on top of the weapon.

DON'T MISS THESE
ALL-ACTION WESTERN SERIES
FROM THE BERKLEY PUBLISHING GROUP

THE GUNSMITH by J. R. Roberts
Clint Adams was a legend among lawmen, outlaws, and ladies. They called him . . . the Gunsmith.

LONGARM by Tabor Evans
The popular long-running series about Deputy U.S. Marshal Custis Long—his life, his loves, his fight for justice.

SLOCUM by Jake Logan
Today's longest-running action Western. John Slocum rides a deadly trail of hot blood and cold steel.

BUSHWHACKERS by B. J. Lanagan
An action-packed series by the creators of Longarm! The rousing adventures of the most brutal gang of cutthroats ever assembled—Quantrill's Raiders.

DIAMONDBACK by Guy Brewer
Dex Yancey is Diamondback, a Southern gentleman turned con man when his brother cheats him out of the family fortune. Ladies love him. Gamblers hate him. But nobody pulls one over on Dex . . .

WILDGUN by Jack Hanson
The blazing adventures of mountain man Will Barlow—from the creators of Longarm!

TEXAS TRACKER by Tom Calhoun
J.T. Law: the most relentless—and dangerous—manhunter in all Texas. Where sheriffs and posses fail, he's the best man to bring in the most vicious outlaws—for a price.

TABOR EVANS

LONGARM

AND THE
GREAT DIVIDE

JOVE BOOKS, NEW YORK

THE BERKLEY PUBLISHING GROUP
Published by the Penguin Group
Penguin Group (USA) LLC
375 Hudson Street, New York, New York 10014

USA • Canada • UK • Ireland • Australia • New Zealand • India • South Africa • China

penguin.com

A Penguin Random House Company

LONGARM AND THE GREAT DIVIDE

A Jove Book / published by arrangement with the author

For information, address: The Berkley Publishing Group,
a division of Penguin Group (USA) LLC,
375 Hudson Street, New York, New York 10014.

ISBN: 978-0-515-15432-0

PUBLISHING HISTORY
Jove mass-market edition / March 2014

PRINTED IN THE UNITED STATES OF AMERICA

10 9 8 7 6 5 4 3 2 1

Cover illustration by Milo Sinovcic.

Chapter 1

"We'll take the Denver and Rio Grande down to Colorado Springs, then an omnibus over to Manitou. I've already wired ahead for a room at Bailey's. It's a bed-an'-breakfast. Very nice. Come evening we'll eat on the pavilion at this French restaurant I know there. It's built beside the creek. You can hear the water chuckle over the rocks. They went an' placed rocks in the creek bed just for the sound, an' it's nice, no question about that. An' the food?" Custis Long rolled his eyes and smiled. Then he leaned a little closer and licked Deborah's left nipple.

"Then come morning, we'll send a boy over to the stable, tell them t' send a buggy for us. They'll drive us through what they call Garden of the Gods. You'll understand why when you see it." He sucked briefly on the left nipple, then switched his attentions to the other pink protrusion. "Beautiful," he said. "Prettiest damn tits in all of Colorado."

"Have you looked at all of them to qualify yourself to make that statement?" Deborah teased.

"Almost," he said with a laugh. "I'm workin' on getting a gander at the rest of 'em."

"What time will you pick me up tomorrow?" Deborah asked as she nuzzled the side of his neck and poked her tongue into his ear.

"'Bout nine," he said, reaching for her bush and sliding a finger into her. "The train leaves at ten forty-five, so that gives us plenty o' time to drive to the station."

Deborah wrapped the fingers of her right hand around his cock. She squeezed affectionately and slipped her tongue into his mouth. "Oh, but that's tomorrow," she whispered, pulling away an inch or so. "Right now . . . more interesting . . ."

An hour or so later, Long left the lady's bed. He stood and stretched to his full six-foot-plus height. Ran a hand over his dark brown hair and smoothed the points of his thick, handlebar mustache.

It always amazed him that the ladies seemed to find him attractive. He did not consider himself to be particularly handsome with his golden brown eyes and craggy features.

He was lean, with a horseman's narrow hips and long, powerful legs set beneath broad shoulders.

Long dressed quickly in brown corduroy trousers and a checked shirt, then sat on the edge of Deborah's bed to pull on black, calf-high cavalry boots. He stood and stamped his feet to settle them into the leather, then buckled his gun belt on, the double-action .45 Colt rigged for a cross draw just to the left of his belt buckle.

He buttoned his vest and reached for his flat-crowned, brown Stetson hat before bending down to give Deborah a good-night kiss. "Nine o'clock," he reminded her.

"I'll be ready. You can count on me, dear."

"Good girl," he said with an affectionate pat on her ass.

The deputy United States marshal let himself out and hailed a hansom cab to take him back to his boardinghouse near Cherry Creek in Denver, Colorado.

When he got into his room and lighted his bedside lamp he found an envelope that had been slipped beneath his door.

"Shit," he muttered aloud when he read the contents.

EMERGENCY. LEAVE CANCELLED.
COME IN.

There was no signature but he recognized the scrawled initials as belonging to his boss, United States marshal William Vail. That meant the note had been written some time after the marshal's chief clerk left for the night.

Emergency, it said. If Billy Vail was calling it that, then it damn sure was an emergency. Billy was not much given to hysterics. The boss was no pencil-pushing political appointee. He was a former Texas Ranger and a salty gent when it came to gunfire. And if he said something was an emergency, well, Longarm was prepared to believe it.

He stripped and sat on the side of his bed. He was tired but before sleeping took the time to clean his revolver and replace the cartridges in it with ammunition fresh from a new box. Billy Vail's emergencies tended to need the application of hot lead to resolve them, and Longarm wanted to be prepared for whatever this one required.

In the morning he headed for the office early. He did not give a thought to Deborah and his plan to take her away for a long weekend, did not even remember her until the day was half gone, long after that nine o'clock promise to meet.

Chapter 2

Longarm was at the office in the Federal Building on Colfax Avenue by seven, so early that Henry was not yet at his desk. But Billy Vail was, bent over his desk with papers spread out before him. Vail looked up in surprise when his best deputy walked in at that hour; Longarm was late more often than not. And now he was coming in at that hour.

"What are you doing here so early?" the boss asked.

"Your note said it was an emergency. So what's up?" Longarm asked in return.

"Oh, I didn't mean . . . I'm sorry if I misled you there. I didn't mean like an immediate, um, *emergency* sort of emergency. I mean something has come up and everyone else is already out on other assignments, so I have to postpone your leave." Vail gave him a rather sheepish smile. "Sorry, Custis."

"Hell, Billy, if I'd knowed that I would've slept another hour or so." Longarm plopped into one of the pair of armchairs arranged in front of Vail's desk. "So what is this non-emergency emergency o' yours?"

Vail shuffled through a slim stack of papers, found the one he wanted, and pulled it out.

"This came in from a town called Valstone, Wyoming

Territory. Frankly I'm not familiar with the community, but they are requesting federal assistance with their local law enforcement. That is entirely within their rights. Apparently they are not capable of handling whatever the problem is up there. They don't specify exactly what that problem is, but they are asking that a company of deputy marshals be sent as quickly as possible."

Billy stood and turned to peer out of the window behind his desk. "Like I told you," he said without looking around, "everyone else is already out on assignment. I know we owe you your accumulated vacation days, and I hate to ask this of you, but . . . I need for you to delay your time off. Go to this Valstone place. See what their problem is and take care of it, please, Custis."

Please, Longarm thought. If the boss was saying "please," then it must be serious.

There was no question of if he would comply with the request. For one thing, it was his duty, plain and simple. For another—and more important—if Billy Vail asked it, Custis Long would do it. He would walk through fire if that was what the boss wanted of him.

"You don't know what their problem is?" he asked.

Vail turned around to face Longarm and shook his head. "No, Custis, I don't. But Wyoming is a territory of the United States of America, and we are charged with preserving the laws of this country. Further, any duly incorporated town, village, or city within the bounds of the country can ask for our assistance. Which these folks have. Now it is up to us to help them."

"Any idea where it is or how I'm t' get there?" Longarm asked.

Vail shrugged. "I was hoping you knew of it."

"I don't." He grinned. "But I reckon I will know soon enough."

Longarm stood and stretched, yawning. "Seein' as how this particular emergency ain't as needful as an orphanage burnin' down, I think I'll go have me some breakfast before I grab my gear an' head up to Wyoming. The boys at the post office in Cheyenne oughta know how I can find Valstone since they'll be directing mail to it. Wherever the hell it is."

"Thank you for doing this, Custis," Billy said.

Longarm grabbed his hat and settled it onto his head. He laughed. "I'll let you know if I need the rest o' this company o' deputies, Billy."

"Right," Vail said. "Just tell me how many you need. I'll be sure to send them. Dozens if you need that many."

"Excuse me now, Boss. I got work t' do. An' grub t' surround." He turned and ambled toward the door at a pace much slower and more relaxed than his arrival had been.

Chapter 3

The post office in Cheyenne was a block and a half from the Union Pacific railroad depot. Longarm left his gear with the station agent at the depot and walked over to the post office. He got there in the middle of the afternoon and asked for the postmaster.

"Do you have an appointment?" the mail clerk asked in return.

"No. I just got in from Denver an' need t' see the gentleman," Longarm said.

"Sorry. Mr. Branscomb only sees people by appointment. If you want to ask for an appointment, I have a form you can fill out and mail in. Would you like a form, sir?"

Longarm sighed. And pulled out his wallet, flipping it open to display his badge. "This is official business, an' I shouldn't need no damn appointment for that."

The clerk scowled. "Why didn't you say so in the first place? Mr. Branscomb's office is in the back. Here. I'll show you."

Branscomb turned out to be a portly fellow probably in his sixties with a fringe of white hair rimming a completely bald pate. He did not look terribly busy. But then Longarm admitted that he did not know much about the business of moving and delivering mail, so it was possible that Branscomb was doing exactly what he was supposed to.

"Come in, Deputy. Sit down. What can I do for you?"

"I need to get to this Valstone place," Longarm told him, "an' I don't have the least idea where it is. What I'm hoping . . . and assuming . . . is that you can point me to it."

Branscomb looked up at the clerk who had brought Longarm to see him. "Get Robert Bortz for me, Lewis."

"Yes, sir."

To Longarm, Branscomb said, "Bortz is in charge of distribution after the mails come in off the trains. He will know where Valstone is, I can assure you, deputy."

Bortz was a small man in his forties or thereabouts. He wore spectacles and sleeve garters. When Longarm's request was put before him, Bortz frowned. "Valstone, you said?"

"That's right." Longarm spelled it for him.

Bortz shook his head. "I'm sorry, but I don't know of any such place."

"But this letter said . . ."

"Was there a postmark?"

It was Longarm's turn to shake his head. "I didn't see the envelope. Marshal Vail showed me the letter but not the envelope."

"Well, someone has certainly made a mistake, Deputy. I am familiar with every post office in the territory of Wyoming, and I can assure you there is none called Valstone."

"That's damn strange," Longarm said.

"Do know where this Valstone is supposed to be?" Bortz asked.

"Not really," Longarm said. "Out on the grass, I think. At least that was the impression my boss had. An' in the east."

Bortz shook his head again. "No, sir. No Valstone. The closest name I can think of is Valmere, though some pronounce it Valmer. Valmere is a small office out on the prairie. Mail service once a week. There is, come to think of it, a town in Nebraska close by Valmere. That is

Stonecipher. I don't know much about it except that it is close to Valmere. Mail going to Stonecipher can be routed through Valmere. Most unusual, but that is the directive we received."

"Does that help you, deputy?" Branscomb asked.

"T' tell you the truth, I don't know if it does." He looked at Bortz and asked, "D'you know how I can get to this Valmere place?"

"Not really, but I can tell you which stagecoach line carries the mail pouches there. Will that help?"

Chapter 4

"No, sir, the way it works," the stage line supervisor explained, "we carry the mail pouch for Valmer once a week on Thursdays. The postmaster for Valmer sends a wagon to meet our coach. Our driver transfers the bag to the Valmer wagon, and that's the end of our responsibility. I don't know where this Valmer actually is. Somewhere east of our line. I'm pretty sure about that, but exactly where . . . ?" The man shrugged. ". . . I wouldn't know."

"And your line runs north from here?" Longarm asked.

"That's right. North through Torrington, Hat Creek, Newcastle, on to Lead and Deadwood."

"So you run pretty close to the territorial boundaries," Longarm said.

"Exactly."

"And Valmer is east of your line."

"I believe so," the stagecoach supervisor said. "At least that's the impression I have from our drivers. Like I say, I've never been there myself and I don't believe any of our drivers have been, either."

"Where does the wagon from Valmer meet your coaches?" Longarm asked.

"There's a layover spot between Lusk and the Hat Creek

station," the supervisor said. "The Valmer wagon is always there waiting on Thursdays. The driver knows to keep the Valmer pouch in his office—"

"You mean in the driving box?" Longarm interrupted.

"That's right. He knows to keep it up top with him, not locked in the luggage boot. He keeps it up there by his feet. Comes the switch, he tosses the Valmer pouch down to whoever is driving the wagon and collects their outgoing pouch, and away he drives. I understand it only takes a few seconds to make the exchange."

"What about passengers?" Longarm asked. "What if there's a passenger bound for Valmer?"

The local man snorted. "You know, now that I think of it, I don't believe we've ever had a passenger ticketed to Valmer. I suppose we could carry them. As far as the transfer point anyway. I don't know how they'd manage from there. On the Valmer wagon, I would imagine, but our ticket wouldn't entitle them to a transfer. We don't have any reciprocal agreement with whoever runs that wagon from Valmer, so . . . I really don't know what to tell you about that, Deputy. A human person wanting to make that transfer, well, he'd be on his own, taking a chance that the Valmer wagon would agree to carry him. And he'd be up shit creek without a paddle if they wouldn't let him board."

"You run coaches up that way daily?" Longarm asked.

The gentleman nodded. "Of course we do."

"Today's coach has already gone?"

"Hours ago." The gent smiled. "But there will be another pulling out at six o'clock tomorrow morning."

"Six?"

"Sharp."

"I'll be there," Longarm said.

"Tomorrow isn't Thursday so there won't be any wagon from Valmer."

"Doesn't matter. I'll figure it out." Longarm touched the brim of his Stetson in salute and left the stage line office.

Chapter 5

Longarm collected his bag from the UP depot and took a room in a cheap hotel close to the tracks. He would only need the bed for a few hours so he saw no need to hire anything fancier.

He quickly washed away the soot gathered from sitting behind a coal-fired engine all day, then dressed and went downstairs.

"Where can I get a decent meal?" he asked the desk clerk.

"Mister, there's cafés all up and down Front Street. There's a good one right on the corner over there," the fellow said, pointing.

"And a quiet saloon?"

The clerk laughed. "Quiet? Sir, I'm not sure there's any such of a thing anywhere in Cheyenne, so take your pick and take your chances. One is about the same as another."

Longarm thanked the man and headed across the street and into the next block to the café the man pointed out. It proved to be more than adequate for his needs, serving beefsteak covered with gravy and a heap of fried potatoes to go with it.

He ate a leisurely meal, paid thirty-five cents for the privilege, and walked half a block to a likely looking saloon.

The saloon was popular enough. It had a piano man, three bartenders, and half a dozen fairly decent-looking whores working the place. There were also four tables with card games in progress. Longarm could not tell just from looking if there were house dealers in the games or if they were open to the players.

"My kinda place," he muttered under his breath as he approached the bar.

His entry was noticed immediately. The nearest bartender slid down his way. "What will you have, mister?"

"Do you have rye whiskey?"

"Of course we do," the man said in a tone of voice that suggested it would be uncivilized to not carry rye.

"I'll have a glass," Longarm said.

"This is a bit house, mister. If you're expecting to want more than one you should go ahead and get the second drink now. It would save you a little. Fifteen cents for one drink or two bits for the two."

Longarm smiled. "I'll have the two, thank you."

The barman dexterously picked up two shot glasses in one hand and a bottle in the other. He quickly filled the pair of glasses and set them down in front of Longarm. A quarter Longarm placed onto the bar disappeared just as quickly into the man's apron pocket.

He turned, leaning against the bar while he surveyed the card games, thinking an evening of low stakes poker would be relaxing.

He savored his first drink. The rye was smooth and pleasant on the tongue and warmed his belly nicely once it hit bottom. Longarm took a minute with the drink, enjoying it slowly.

The second table in, he decided. The men who were already playing seemed a congenial bunch. No one was in the game for the money, rather for the pleasure of the play, or so it looked.

Longarm finished his first glass and turned back to the bar for the second.

The glass was there, but the whiskey was gone.

Some son of a bitch had stolen Custis Long's whiskey!

"Cocksucking son of a bitch," Longarm roared loud enough to stop the piano player in mid-piece, loud enough to rattle the rafters.

He took half a step back and grabbed the two men who were standing to his right and to his left. Grabbed them by the scruff of the neck, one in each powerful hand, and demanded, "All right, you bastards, which one o' you drank my whiskey?"

His answer came in the form of flying fists.

Chapter 6

The fellow on Longarm's left, a railroad man judging by his clothing, threw a hard underhand punch into Longarm's belly. Longarm saw it coming and tensed his muscles. The belligerent might as well have hit a wooden plank. He grimaced and looked down at his hand to see if it was injured.

Meanwhile Longarm squared off and planted a hard right onto the jaw of the big bastard to his right. That one was rocked backward, his lip split and blood beginning to flow.

Longarm encouraged that seepage by following his right with a left hand that pulped the big fellow's nose, splattering blood in all directions.

By that time the saloon full of drinkers had degenerated into a wild melee of fists, curses and not a few kicks.

The bartenders moved quickly to drop a heavy canvas drape over the backbar mirror. They put it in place barely in time as the glassware was beginning to fly, not a few of the missiles thumping onto the canvas.

The two bartenders at the ends of the bar then moved with equal speed to grab up bungstarters and stand guard at the two entrances to the cockpit behind the bar, there to ward off any attempts to slip in and steal a bottle or two.

Longarm ducked under a punch aimed toward his face

and countered with right-left-right into the fellow's gut. A
fist came at him out of nowhere. It crunched into his jaw
and knocked him off balance for a moment.

The first man he had hit was floored by someone club-
bing him with a whiskey bottle while the gent with the broken nose decked a lanky cowboy. In the center of the room
a gentleman, apparently an Englishman in top hat and tails,
held his own using his cane like a sword.

The battle raged for perhaps three minutes until the
effects of adrenaline overcame those of alcohol and people
began thinking more about limiting the damage to themselves than they did about their zeal to punch the hell out of
someone else.

Things quickly came under control then.

Longarm leaned down and helped the big fellow with the
broken nose to his feet.

"Thank you, sir," the big man said, his grin exposing a
mouth that held fewer teeth than God intended.

"It's the least I could do," Longarm said. "I hope you
don't mind me mentionin' it, but you are still bleeding."

"Yeah, once this nose starts it don't stop real easy."

Longarm motioned to the nearest bartender. "I need a bit
of paper. Something about the size of a postage stamp will do."

The barman looked at him like he thought Longarm had
gone off his rocker, but he found a receipt book and tore the
corner off of a sheet.

Longarm rolled the paper into as tight a cylinder as he
could manage and handed it to the big man. "Stick this
between your teeth and your upper lip. It'll stop the nose-
bleed."

"How the hell?"

Longarm shrugged. "Damn if I know, but it's a trick a doc
taught me once. It works a charm, too."

"If you say so." The fellow stuffed the paper into his
mouth.

"Tuck it up there good an' tight," Longarm encouraged.

Moments later the big man crowed. "Damn! I ain't bleeding now."

"Like I said. Works a charm, that trick."

"Say now, I sure owe you for this." He gave Longarm a sheepish look and added, "Fact is, I drank your whiskey, that started this whole thing. Thought it was mine."

"Think nothing of it, neighbor. Can I buy you another?" Longarm asked.

"Aw, I think it's my turn to buy you one," the big man said. He stuck his hand out to shake, saying, "The name is Mike Sample."

"Custis Long," Longarm said, taking Sample's hand and giving it a firm shake. "Belly up to the bar, Mike. We'll see if we can drink in peace for a little while. Then maybe you'd fancy a turn with the cards."

"That I would, Custis Long," Sample said.

By the end of that evening—and a bottle and a half of rye whiskey—Longarm and Sample were best friends forever.

But in the morning Longarm's head ached along with his jaw.

Chapter 7

Longarm was feeling considerably better by the time the coach pulled into Lusk for a quick change of horses. The sun was slanting low and the wind was picking up. The passengers in the coach were in for a long, cold night.

"I'll be leaving you here," Longarm told the driver. "Any suggestions about where a man could find a decent room?" The prospects did not look great, not from looking around the town.

The driver pointed to a building in the next block. "You'll want to stay at the Drover's Rest there."

"It's good?" Longarm asked.

The driver grinned and said, "It's the only."

Longarm laughed. "In that case . . ." He picked up his bag and began hiking up the street toward the Drover's Rest.

After a sound sleep—disturbed not more than a dozen times by the hatmaker's supplies salesman he was required to share the bed with—Longarm had a hot breakfast and a cigar and pronounced himself fit for the day.

"I need t' hire a horse," he told the gent at the café. "Where might I find one?"

"Only place in town that rents stock would be the livery,"

the café owner said. "You can find it behind the stage stop yonder." The man pointed, then used that finger to scratch his balls. Longarm was pleased that he had finished his meal *before* seeing that.

Longarm grabbed his bag and headed back toward the stagecoach station where his bedmate from the previous night was engaged in buying a ticket for points south.

Just as claimed, there was a tall, solidly built barn behind the stage depot. The place looked to be more soundly built and considerably quieter than the Drover's Rest had been, but it was a little too late to discover that now, otherwise he might have elected to curl up in a pile of hay rather than share bed time with a stranger. Particularly with a stranger who seemed to possess a bladder the size of a peanut.

The livery's corral held a collection of heavy-bodied cobs, likely the property of the stagecoach line and kept in rotation for pulling the coach. Several of those were handsome animals, but none of them was of interest to Longarm.

"I'm needing a good saddle horse," Longarm told the hostler when the man showed up, an empty feed bucket in one hand and a curry comb in the other.

"Rent or buy?" the skinny old man asked.

"Rent," Longarm said.

"I got one I could let out. For a price, of course. Up to you if you think he's 'good.' I don't make no claims about that."

"Drag him out here then," Longarm said. "I'll take him."

"You ain't seen him yet."

"Doesn't matter. I got t' have a saddle horse for a few days so I'll take him regardless."

The hostler turned his head and spat. "Wait here, mister. I'll be right back with your horse."

"Saddle, too, o' course," Longarm said.

"I got two. They're yonder," the hostler said, pointing. "Take your pick."

While the liveryman was out in the corrals fetching in

the saddle horse, Longarm looked over the saddles. And concluded that if the horse was as bad as the worn-out saddles, he was in for a long day.

The horse, as it turned out, was not nearly as good as the saddles.

It was going to be a long day.

Chapter 8

The day got longer and even less pleasant as he was approaching the wide spot where he assumed the stagecoaches pulled aside to meet the Thursday wagon from Valmere.

There were already two men there, saddles loosed, giving their horses a break while both man and animal had a drink, the horses drinking water from Hat Creek and the men quenching their thirst from a whiskey shared bottle.

"Howdy." Longarm nodded and dismounted, glad to get off both the miserable saddle and the even worse horse. He led the stupid son of a bitch of a gelding to the thread of cool water and let the horse have its head so it could drink if it wanted to. Not that that was likely; the horse had not wanted to do much of anything Longarm suggested so far, so why should it start now?

He stretched, arching his back, then removed his coat and tied it on top of his carpetbag strapped behind the cantle of the livery saddle.

The two men got up from where they had been lounging on a patch of tall grass. There was something about the way they were looking at him . . .

"Well, shit," Longarm mumbled as he slipped beneath

the rented horse's neck so the animal was between him and the travelers.

"Mister," the taller of the two called as they came near.

That one wore a derby hat and a sack coat. He had about a week's growth of dark beard and had run-down boots.

His companion was very slightly shorter and very slightly the better dressed of the two, wearing a tailored coat, bright bandanna, and wide-brimmed boss-of-the-plains hat crimped in a Montana peak.

Both men wore pistols hanging at their bellies.

Longarm peered at them over the back of his seal brown horse. "Ayuh?"

"We was wondering if you could help us out," the shorter one said.

"Prob'ly not," Longarm told them. "I don't know this country worth a damn. Just trying t' get to a place called Valmer or maybe it's Valmere. Anyway, I need t' get there, but I ain't from around here and wouldn't know enough t' give directions."

"No, it ain't directions we're looking for." The tall one glanced at the short one and both of them grinned a little.

The short one looked at Longarm and said, "What we had in mind was for you to help us with whatever money you got on you."

"*All* of whatever money you got," the tall one said.

Longarm sighed. "I don't think so."

"Mind now, we did ask polite," the short one said.

Both of them reached to take out their pistols.

"You're making a mistake." Longarm told them. "A pretty bad mistake, so give this up before you get hurt."

"Mister, let me remind you, we are two guns to your one, so you give it up before we hurt you."

"Mister, may I inform you that your guns are in your leather while my .45 is right here in my hand."

"Mister, I think you're lying."

Longarm rested his left arm on his saddle while he leaned

against the horse as it drank, head down, ears flapping back and forth while it swallowed.

He waited, hoping the two would give up their bad idea to rob a passing stranger and go back to their whiskey bottle. Hoping, but not really expecting.

He was right not to hope for a peaceful resolution to this little problem. The two idiots dragged iron.

Longarm gave the men time to reconsider while they took aim at his head, which was all that was exposed over the back of the brown horse.

Then the shooting started, and the two gents had run out of time.

Chapter 9

Longarm dropped behind the brown horse, ducked low, and reemerged beneath the animal's neck.

His .45 bellowed, and the brown's head came up as the horse reared onto its hind legs.

Longarm fired again, taking the man on the right first, the smaller of the two. The son of a bitch would not go down so Longarm shot him a third time. He was positive his bullets flew true, but the little man simply refused to drop.

There was no time to fool with him any further for the taller one was shooting now. Longarm could hear the bumblebee drone of the slugs passing close by his head. He threw a hasty shot at the taller one and shot the short man a fourth time, that slug finally dropping him.

Longarm stood up, took careful aim and squeezed off a sixth . . . nothing.

His hammer fell on an empty chamber. In the heat of the moment he had forgotten that he was carrying only five cartridges in his Colt, this in case the livery horse gave him grief and made his .45 fall out of the leather.

Men have been known to shoot themselves—sometimes fatally—in just that manner, a revolver hammer striking the ground and in turn hitting the cartridge primer. That can be funny when the accidental shot hits no one; it can be tragic when the errant bullet strikes flesh.

Now Longarm had an empty gun and a pissed-off opponent not twenty feet away.

The man in the derby hat and black sack coat blasted nervously in Longarm's general direction, his bullets flying high until his gun, too, was empty.

Derby looked at Longarm, saw the lawman was out of ammunition, and reached for a knife.

Longarm also hauled a knife out, his a folding lockblade that he kept sharp enough for the occasional shave. He snapped it open and stepped around behind the brown horse.

"You killed my partner, you son of a bitch," Derby snapped, his face contorting like he was close to breaking out in tears.

Longarm stood his ground, waiting to see if Derby was any better with a knife than with a gun.

Unfortunately he was. He dropped into a crouch and crept crabwise toward Longarm, staying low with his knife hand extended and a wide grin splitting his face.

It would have been a fine time to have a cartridge or three remaining in the Colt but what he had was a folding pocketknife and a determination that this grinning piece of shit was not going to gut him and leave his body beside a shallow creek in eastern Wyoming Territory.

Beside Longarm the brown horse coughed and went down to its knees. He would have gone to it to see if there was any way he could give it ease, but his attention was—and had to be—fixed on Derby. And on the man's wicked knife blade.

Derby came in closer, still grinning, still crouched low, still with blood in his eye.

Longarm waited. Weighed the familiar heft of his knife. Knew it came up short against the belt knife Derby wielded.

The thing about a knife fight is that they are sudden things, over almost as quickly as they begin. Longarm expected this one to be no different. He would pit his speed and determination against that of Derby.

And one of them would die.

Derby shuffled closer. Closer still.

The man's knife hand lashed out toward Longarm's belly.

And in less than a second the fight was over.

Chapter 10

"You black-hearted, cocksucking bastard," Derby groaned. "You've killed me, haven't you."

Longarm hunkered down beside the man. He took out a cheroot and lighted it, remembering to offer it first to the man on the ground. Finally he nodded. "Ayuh, reckon I have."

The haft of Longarm's knife protruded just beneath Derby's breastplate. The blade extended up under the ribs and probably pierced the lower end of the man's heart.

Longarm had suffered a razor-thin cut on the inside of his left bicep. If he had been wearing his coat, he thought, he would have escaped injury completely.

"How . . . how long?" Derby asked.

"Not long," Longarm said. "Couple minutes maybe. Are you wanted for anything?"

"No, this . . . this was our first stickup."

"You should've stuck to herding cows."

"Will you have us buried proper?" Derby asked.

"I'm on official business, but I'll leave word. D'you have paper an' pencil?"

"I do. In my right-hand saddlebag. Will you see that we have markers, me and my pard?"

"That I will. It's why I asked for paper an' pencil."

"My name is Chester Thomas Teegarten. My partner there is Wil Canby. That's Wilford."

Teegarten was growing pale as the blood leaked from him, and his voice was weak. The man was still in his right mind, but he only had moments left, Longarm thought.

Longarm stayed beside him, smoking his cheroot, until Teegarten drew his last breath.

Then Longarm stood and went to the horses Teegarten and Canby had ridden to this spot. He rummaged through their saddlebags until he found the promised paper and pencil and wrote out a note saying he had killed them in the line of duty and they should be buried at government expense. He gave their names and a brief description so each body could be properly identified—not that he supposed it really made much of a difference now which marker went over which grave—and tucked the note into Teegarten's pocket.

He took a few more moments to drag the bodies to the side of the road where the next coach through would see them.

There was nothing he could do for the hired brown horse. The next time he was through Lusk he would give the livery man a voucher to pay for the miserable beast. Then he unsaddled and turned loose the poorer of the horses Teegarten and Canby had been riding. He tightened the cinch on the better of the two, a likely looking gray with good butt and wide stance in front, and transferred his gear to that horse.

He stepped onto the gray and touched it with his heels, guiding the animal onto the thin track left by the wagon that came once a week to collect the mail pouch for Valmere, Wyoming Territory. The horse splashed across the shallow stream that might—or might not—have been Hat Creek and headed east at a comfortable lope.

Chapter 11

"What the fuck?" Longarm blurted aloud when he saw the signs that flanked the road.

A hundred yards or so back the track had taken a sharp turn to the north. Now he was confronted by this pair of signs. The one on the left read VALMERE, WYO. TERR. and the sign on the right read STONECIPHER, NEBRASKA.

The town that lay beyond them was equally split, left and right. One general mercantile on the left and another, almost-identical store facing it across the wide road. The false front of a saloon was on the left and another, almost-identical saloon facing it across the road on the right side.

Beyond the stores were equally similar smithies, each with a public corral attached. Aside from those there were a scant few houses on either side of the road.

The road itself widened here so there was room for normal traffic to pass on either side of a line of stakes that were driven down the middle of the roadway.

"What the fuck?" Longarm repeated to himself as he entered . . . he was not entirely sure if he was riding into Valmere, Wyoming Territory . . . or Stonecipher, Nebraska. Or both.

Valstone, the message back in Billy Vail's office said it

was from. Valstone. Valmere plus Stonecipher apparently
equaled Valstone.

Longarm rode into town—or the towns, plural—on the
Wyoming side of the markers, past the storefronts to the blacksmith's shop. He reined to a halt and dismounted there.

The smithy, a smallish, wiry man with dark hair and
powerful arms, stepped out to make a very obvious inspec-
tion of the gray horse. After a moment he said, "You ride a
Cutrell horse but you don't dress like no Cutrell man. Who
are you and what are you doing on this side of the divide?"

"Pardon me?"

"I said . . ."

"Oh, I heard you, mister, but I don't understand what
you're sayin'," Longarm explained. "First off, I don't know
anybody named Cutrell. The horse is one I was left with after
the fella that had been on it killed my animal. An' who I ride
for is the U.S. government. I'm the deputy marshal someone
here sent for."

The blacksmith broke into a broad smile. He snapped his
fingers and did a little jig. "Hot damn. We're finally going
to settle this thing. We'll finally get rid of those sons o'
bitches."

"Uh, exactly what sons o' bitches would you be talkin'
about?" Longarm asked.

"Why, them sons o' bitches across the way, of course."
The blacksmith waved in the general direction of Nebraska.

"The sons . . ."

"Bastards stole our town. Stole the location, anyhow. As
you can plainly see for your own self." Again the smith
waved across the broad street toward Nebraska. "This here
is a Wyoming town. We want you to make those Cutrell
and Sagamore and Gleason bastards take their town someplace else."

"Look, this is all kinda confusing," Longarm said.
"How's about I unsaddle this Cutrell horse . . . whatever
that's s'posed to mean . . . an' find a place for both him an'

me to stay for a spell. Can you board this horse for me, mister? Even if it is a Cutrell horse?"

"Oh, sure, I can do that. He can stand in my corral along with the others." The smith grunted. "I expect the horses won't know the difference when I put him in among them."

Longarm unstrapped his carpetbag from behind the cantle of what had been Chester Teegarten's saddle and loosened the cinch of the gray. He draped the saddle over a rail of the corral fence and led the gray inside to get at the hay and water available there.

"Any idea where I might put up?" he asked the smith.

The man seemed to find the question amusing but after a moment he said, "Generally the fellas who show up here want mostly two things. And sleep ain't either one of them. But maybe you could have a bed in Stella's whorehouse yonder. It's the biggest house this side of the street." He pointed and grinned. "God knows they got beds there but I doubt there's ever been anybody using one of them just to sleep in."

"There's noplace else?" Longarm asked.

"Not that I can think of," the blacksmith said. "They're nice folks at Stella's, though. Give them a try. Then get about the business of kicking out those sons o' bitches across the street."

Longarm picked up his bag and headed off in the direction the smith had indicated, still not sure just what the hell he was doing here.

Chapter 12

"We aren't open yet, mister. Just you keep it in your pants for another little while. We be open by and by."

"This is a different kind of business I have in mind," Longarm said. He showed his badge and explained the problem. "So what I'm looking for is room an' board. The government will pay," he concluded, peering down at the plump little black woman who had opened the door.

She brightened when she saw the badge. "You here to throw those bastards out? Well, you just come in and set yourself down. Take any room you want. You say your name is Long? Well, welcome, Marshal Long. You stay here long as you like. My name is Hettie and I take good care of you, me and my girls will. Then when you ready we go over to the saloon. You meet everybody. They be as happy to see you as I is."

Hettie grabbed at his bag, practically wrestling him for it, then scampered ahead of him up the staircase.

"This our best room," she said, pausing at a door. "If it be all right, you move in. Stay long as you like."

Up and down the corridor doors were being opened and heads were poking out to see who was there. Female heads, the girls with tousled hair and without makeup. Without the gaudy face paint and ribbons they looked like a bunch of schoolgirls.

Hettie deposited Longarm's carpetbag on the foot of a low, sturdy bed and said, "Come downstairs when you ready. I take you over to the saloon. Introduce you to everybody. All right?"

"Just fine," he assured her.

Hettie bobbed her head and backed out of the room, closing the door as she went.

Longarm shrugged and looked around the accommodation. It was not exactly a high-class hotel room, but it would do. There was no wardrobe, just a series of hooks on the wall, and a washstand beneath them.

He moved his bag to the floor and unfastened the straps that held it closed, the act being enough to make him feel that he had moved in.

With another shrug he went back downstairs to find Hettie and meet "everybody" in Val . . . uh . . . Valstone, Wyobraska.

Chapter 13

"Welcome, Marshal, welcome indeed. We all heard you were here." The gentleman laughed and said, "We knew Hettie would bring you over to meet us, so we all got together so we could meet you, you see. This is, um, this is every single resident of Valmere, Wyoming. Every one. Not counting the cowhands who come and go, of course."

"And not counting wives," someone put in from the back of the bunch. "Some of us do have wives here."

"And some of us probably have wives back East, but we don't talk about them," another voice said, prompting a round of laughter from the others.

There were not a dozen men—and Hettie, of course—in the place. The permanent population of the town. Or at least representing the Wyoming half of the town, Longarm noted.

"I'm Jacob Potts," the first gent said, extending his hand.

"And I'm George Griner. I'm Jake's bartender," another offered.

"You already met me. Well, sort of," the blacksmith said. "I'm Otis Reed."

They moved in close to introduce themselves, shake hands and fade back again, one by one until Longarm had met every businessman—businessperson, that is, including Hettie—in Valmere, Wyoming Territory. But not a soul from across the street in Stonecipher, Nebraska.

Longarm was beginning to wonder if there *were* people who lived on the Nebraska side of this borderline burg. He had yet to meet any of them.

"What we want," Potts the saloon owner said, "is for you to send those bastards packing." He motioned to George Griner, who hurried around behind the bar and drew a beer for their guest.

Longarm tasted the beer. It was sour and a little bit flat. "There's a lot o' bastards in the world," he said. "Which particular ones are you wantin' me to get rid of for you?"

It was posed as a question, but he felt sure he already knew the answer to it.

"Why, those sons o' bitches across the way," Potts said.

"We was here first," put in a weasel-faced little man whose name Longarm did not remember.

"We cleaned out the spring," another said.

"We all draw from the same water. It's why the town was put here."

"Uh-huh," Longarm said, sipping at the truly awful brew in his mug.

"They got no business using that water after we're the ones cleaned the spring."

"That government survey crew came through. They ran the territorial boundary right up the middle of our main street," someone complained.

"Right through the middle of the spring, too."

"So now Nebraska claims that water as theirs."

"But everybody knows it's really ours."

It seemed like everyone in the room had an opinion. Not only had one, they all wanted Longarm to hear those opinions.

Longarm set the mug aside still half full. He had not

tasted anything this bad in years. "You wouldn't happen t' have any rye whiskey, would you, Jake?"

"Rye whis . . . what does that have to do with anything?" Potts snapped. Then he blanched and gave Longarm a worried look as if fearful he might have offended the marshal and ruined their chances to get rid of the Nebraska interlopers. "Oh! Rye whiskey," he said, as if he was just now hearing that there was such a thing. "No, sorry, no rye."

"What we have is jug whiskey," Griner said from behind the bar. "Would you like a taste?"

"Jug whiskey? Like you, um, make it here yourselves?" Longarm returned.

"Yes, but the alcohol is all tax paid," Potts quickly said.

"No snake heads?" Longarm asked.

"Oh, no. A little molasses, gunpowder. Water and of course the alcohol. Everything has to be freighted in from Cheyenne and the charges to get distillery whiskey here . . . you wouldn't believe how much that costs." Potts brightened. "Besides, the cowboys who trade here don't seem to mind the difference."

"I'll try a little," Longarm said, skeptical but willing. He for damn sure did not want any more of that cheap beer that Potts was selling.

Hettie tugged at his sleeve and he bent down so she could whisper in his ear, "I have some good whiskey over at the house. I'll give you some of that when you come over for supper."

"Thanks, honey."

"So anyway, Marshal," Potts said, returning to the business at hand, "those bastards across the way are stealing our water. We figure we got rights to that water, and we figure our federal government should see that we get our proper rights."

"That's right," a chorus of approving voices agreed.

Longarm absently picked up the shot glass George Griner

pushed in his direction. As he had begun to half expect, Jacob Potts's so-called jug whiskey was every bit as bad as the man's beer.

He was commencing to sorely miss Denver's many delightful pubs.

Chapter 14

"Thank you for the hospitality, gents, but I need t' go across the street an' talk to those folks now," Longarm said to the room at large. Silently to himself he added: And see if they have any decent beer or rye whiskey.

His announcement drew a round of smiles and great joy.

"You're gonna kick the bastards out, right?"

"Go get them, Marshal."

"Tell them that water is ours."

"Just keep them away from our spring. That will send them packing."

"Great job, Marshal."

Great job? he thought. He hadn't done anything yet. Moreover, he had no idea what he was going to do or even what it was possible to do. All he wanted to do across the street was to meet those folks and see what their side of the story might be.

But it seemed a poor idea to mention any of that to the good folk of Valmere.

Longarm let himself out of the saloon with a chorus of well-wishes following at his backside.

It was a considerable hike across to the Nebraska side of things, each half of the divided street being wide enough for three wagons to pass abreast.

A line of stakes had been pounded into the hard prairie soil smack down the center of the street. To keep delivery wagons from straying over to the "enemy" side? Or cattle? He had no idea what the purpose was. Perhaps it was only to make the residents on either side feel better about it all.

Whatever the purpose it was no barrier. Longarm walked across to the Stonecipher side and stepped up onto the boardwalk in front of the Nebraska saloon.

"Welcome, Deputy Long," someone immediately greeted.

Longarm grinned. It seemed someone in Nebraska was spying on the Wyoming contingent because there was not a familiar face among the—he paused to count—fifteen people in the place.

Those fifteen, however, certainly seemed to know who he was. And the reason he was there.

"Now let us tell you what the truth is," a tall, nearly bald gent said, extending his hand to shake.

Chapter 15

"My name is Potts, deputy. Jason Potts. I own the saloon here." Potts was grinning like he had a secret that Longarm was not privy to.

"Potts. You aren't . . ."

Potts laughed out loud, a deep, hearty belly laugh. And Longarm caught on.

"You and Jacob are brothers," he said, thinking about the saloon owner from across the street on the Wyoming side of things.

"That's right," Jason Potts said, laughing again. "Our pap ran a saloon back in Kentucky. You could say we grew up in the business."

"Then why . . . ?"

"This feud between us?" Potts shrugged. "It just happened." He laughed again. "Sort of."

"How's come you two can't share? I understand it's the spring that you're feuding over, so why can't you just call it a draw and share that water?" Longarm asked.

"It's more than water. It's . . . everything," Potts said. Then his grin flashed again. "Jake and me haven't been able to share, not ever. When we was boys we'd have a dozen toys on the ground between us, but we'd fight over one. We've always been like that."

"They tried to steal our business," one of the men in the group put in. When Longarm raised an eyebrow he added, "They came over here and tried to lure our cowboys away to their side."

"You stake a claim on a particular batch of cowboys?" Longarm asked.

The fellow nodded. "We trade with the Nebraska stockmen and their cowboys. The Double T and R Slash and the Rafter O. They're ours. They're Nebraska brands."

"And over on that side?" Longarm asked.

"They do business with the TTL, the XOX, the MCX, and the XL Bar. They're all Wyoming brands. The thing is, um, the state of Nebraska doesn't recognize Wyoming brands. So any Wyoming beeves that wander across the line could be . . . I'm not saying they necessarily are . . . but those animals could legally be claimed over here."

"And if your livestock wander over there?" Longarm reached for a cheroot. A thin young man in the crowd quickly snapped a match aflame and held it for him.

The question brought a chorus of scowls from the assembled gents. "Then the sons o' bitches steal them," Potts said.

"Ah, so if your beeves stray into Wyoming, that crowd steals them. But if theirs happen t' come over here, then you're only gathering unclaimed stock if you take 'em and run 'em in with your herds."

"Not our herds exactly. We're businessmen not stockmen," Potts said, "but you have the general idea."

"But you have no choice except to share the water since that's the only standing water around here," Longarm said.

"That pretty much explains the way of things," Potts agreed.

"And the letter to Marshal Vail?"

"What letter?" he got back from the Nebraska contingent.

"You boys don't know anything about a letter that came from a place called Valstone?"

"Not me."

"No, sir."

"Not none of us."

"Do you have a post office?" Longarm asked them.

"Our general store has a mail counter in back."

"And across the way?"

"Same thing. It's a mail counter, not exactly a post office. We talked about applying for a regular post office, but we haven't gotten around to it just yet."

"Interesting," Longarm said. He scratched an itch on the side of his nose and smoothed his mustache tips, then dug into his britches for a coin. "I could stand a beer," he said. "Maybe even a beer an' a shot."

"Here, deputy. Let us buy," came the return, a purely lovely sentiment, Longarm thought.

And he was right about at least one thing. The beer and the whiskey in Jason Potts's Nebraska saloon were much better than in Jacob Potts's Wyoming establishment.

Chapter 16

"Hi, everyone. I'm sorry I'm late." The voice came from behind him as he stood with a whiskey glass raised halfway to his lips. The voice was soft and husky and very feminine, and as he turned around he thought . . .

"Oh, God. Liz?"

The lady smiled. "Hello, Custis."

"My God, I can't believe . . . what are you doing here?"

Elizabeth Kunsler said, "Why, I came to the meeting, of course. All the merchants in Stonecipher are invited."

"But . . . you. What are *you* doing here? In the town, I mean. The last time I saw you . . ."

"I was living in Omaha," she finished for him. "I married. You remember James, don't you? James Stonecipher. He discovered this spot and recognized the need for stores to supply the ranches in the area. So he developed the town. Jimmy died last year . . ."

"I'm sorry 'bout that, Liz."

"Don't be. He was a nice man but frankly not everything a woman could want. He did leave me fairly well off, though. I own all of the buildings in Stonecipher now. I live off my rents. And, Custis, when you are done here I would like to speak with you." There was a twinkle in her bright blue eyes when she lowered her voice a notch and added, "In private."

He had known Liz—what was it—five years ago? Six? She was quite the dame then. A handful. Pretty, vivacious, and full of fun.

On their first outing he hired a buggy and drove down along the Missouri. They found a cool, sheltered glade . . . and the first thing out of Liz's mouth was that she was going in for a swim. She did, too. Stripped herself bare as a boiled egg and splashed around in the shallows.

She admitted later that she could not swim a lick. But she did know how to have a good time.

"Soon as we're done here," he told her. "Just tell me where."

Chapter 17

"So who requested federal help with your law enforcement?" Longarm asked. "And why?"

"That is simple enough, Custis," Elizabeth Kunsler told him. "Neither town can afford a full time marshal, and if we did have one there would be the problem of jurisdiction. I mean, a marshal in Stonecipher couldn't arrest a lawbreaker in Valmere and vice versa. A Nebraska lawman has to stop at the state line, don't you see. That is where his authority ends. I assume it is the same over on their side."

"Yet you folks got together enough t' ask for our help," Longarm said.

"And it took two months of very careful negotiation to accomplish that," Potts put in.

"Couple times there we thought we'd come to shooting over who was to do what," a gentleman in sleeve garters and a derby hat said.

"Couple times I wanted to pull a gun on those bastards," another gent said.

"In the end," Potts said, "each side laid out our proposed wording and we pulled one out of a hat to decide."

Longarm looked at Liz and said, "You were always a sensible girl. I'm surprised you couldn't ride herd on 'em."

"Oh, I wasn't permitted in the meetings," she told him. "Something about me being a woman."

He grinned down at her. "Over on the Wyoming side, women have pretty much the same rights as men. Voting an' everything. You did know that didn't you?"

"Yes, but that is over there. This is Nebraska, and women here do not have voting privileges. Or much of anything else."

"Don't start that, Elizabeth," Potts said. To Longarm he added, "Our Elizabeth wants to act like this is Wyoming. It isn't, and we are quite happy with the way our laws run."

Longarm grunted. "What you all need, I think, is a peacemaker."

"Right, and that is where you come in. As a federal marshal you can cross back and forth. With you here a man who shoots up my place can't get away from responsibility for it just by walking across the street. That's all he needs to do the way things are now; he just walks across the street and he's free from arrest.

"Convenient," Longarm said.

"But bad for business," another man put in. "The way it is now, a man can run out on a bill and escape paying just by stepping across that line."

"I can see how that would be a nuisance," Longarm agreed.

"Nuisance be damned. The cowboys all know about it, and some of them deliberately run up their bills over here then scamper across the line to keep from paying what they owe."

"Makes it hard for an honest merchant to turn a profit," said the gentleman Longarm thought he remembered as being the proprietor of the general store on the Stonecipher side of town.

"Or a dishonest one," someone at the back of the room added, which made the storekeeper's head snap back around but too late for him to see who made the comment.

"I think I see the problem," Longarm told the crowd.

"The problem is them," the storekeeper said. "They need to move their town away from us."

"And they need to quit stealing our water. That's another thing. We developed that spring. The water is ours."

"Right. The water belongs to us. We should make them stop using it. That would certainly get some results. Do that and they would have to move away from here."

Longarm looked down at Liz and raised an eyebrow.

"Don't look at me, Custis. I'm just a woman. I have no right to say anything. About anything."

"Frustratin', ain't it," he said.

"You wouldn't know the half of it," she said.

"We'll talk 'bout all o' that later. Right now, I'm hungry. I assume you got a café over on this side," Longarm said.

"No café meal for you this evening," Liz said. "You're coming home with me for supper. We have a lot of catching up to do." She hooked her arm into his and announced, "This meeting is over. I'm taking the deputy home for a good meal. We can worry about business tomorrow."

With that she turned him around and dragged him toward the door.

Chapter 18

Liz's house was a modest bungalow, not the mansion he expected. She held his hand and led him inside. As soon as he closed the door behind them, Liz turned and melted into his arms.

"You feel every bit as good as I remembered," he told her.

She laughed. "And your hard-on feels just like I remember."

Longarm bent his face to hers and kissed her long and deep. "D'you have house help these days?"

"No, why?"

"In that case it'll be all right if I unbutton that dress . . ."

"I can probably get myself out of it quicker than you can manage, Custis. Take care of your own clothes, and let's see who gets naked the quicker."

"Deal," he said and began stripping. Moments later he said, "You win. So what d'you want for your prize?"

Liz looked down at the huge cock that was lightly throbbing in its erection. She laughed again and said, "That. I want that for my prize."

"Then I got no choice. You won it fair an' square," Longarm said. He took her into his arms again and kissed her. When they broke apart he said, "Where?"

She turned and led him through the parlor into a modestly furnished bedroom. Liz had an exceptionally soft feather bed. She sank into it, holding her arms for him to join her.

He did, springs creaking as he stretched out beside her.

Elizabeth Kunsler was slender, no longer a spring chicken but with large, firm tits that seemed even larger on her thin frame. Her waist was tiny. Longarm could practically span it with his two hands.

At the moment, however, it was not her waist that he was thinking of.

He kissed her again, probing her mouth with his tongue, then moved lower, finding an engorged nipple and taking it into his mouth. Liz arched her back, practically pushing her nipple into his mouth as he sucked and teased.

She eased him away from her nipple and gently pushed him onto his back.

"You don't mind?" she asked.

Longarm laughed. "I remember what 'tis that you like, darlin'. Glad to oblige."

He lay there on the softness of the deep feathers while Liz moved to straddle him, facing toward his feet. With a whimper of eagerness she bent to him, first running her tongue around the head of his cock, then taking him into her mouth. Shallow at first. Then deeper. Sucking. Nibbling. Moaning with pleasure of her own as Longarm's tongue flicked over her clitoris.

He buried his tongue in her pussy, tasting the sweet nectar there. Then out again to concentrate on her clitoris.

After what seemed like mere seconds Liz shuddered and stiffened.

"That was quick," he said, pulling away from her pussy far enough that he could speak.

Liz raised her head from his cock, kissed the tip of it and said, "It's been a long time, Custis. I don't want any . . . entanglements in town here. That could be awkward. So I have the reputation of celibacy." She laughed. "If you can believe that."

"Yeah, but I know you better," he said.

Liz could not answer. She had her mouth full of his prick.

Longarm smiled. And resumed licking her pussy until she came a second time. And a third.

And by that time his own sap was rising to the level of explosion, bursting forth in a powerful climax, spewing into Liz's throat.

She drank his come, and he hugged her close.

Chapter 19

Longarm woke slowly, for the moment unsure of where he was. Then memory returned and he smiled. Liz was lying close beside him, curled onto her right side, her back to Longarm.

He reached over and ran his hand lightly over the swell of her rump. He felt a swelling of his own as, thinking about Liz, his cock became engorged.

He rolled onto his side tight against her, his cock slipping in between her legs from behind. Longarm arched his back and slowly slid inside Elizabeth. She made a small sound and reached back to place her hand on his hip.

He kept the rhythm slow and easy, coming after several pleasant minutes. Then he withdrew and leaned forward to kiss her between her shoulder blades.

Liz mumbled something that he could not quite make out. He kissed her again and rolled over, sitting up on the side of the bed and reaching for his clothes.

He was hungry and he knew if he woke Liz, she would get up and cook for him, but there seemed no need for that. Instead, he dressed and quietly let himself out of her bedroom.

It was not yet daylight, but he could see lights in a café

across the way on the Wyoming side. He let himself out into
the chilly predawn, settled his hat comfortably on his head,
and strode out into the darkness.

"Good morning. Are you open for business yet?" He remembered the café owner from the day before but could not
remember the man's name.

The brawny fellow smiled in greeting. "Good morning,
Marshal. I won't be open, not officially anyhow, for another
half hour or so, but I can fix you something now if you like.
Ham steak and fried spuds be all right for you? I can't get
any eggs out this far, but we have plenty potatoes."

"Just fine, thanks."

"The coffee is just starting to boil, so it isn't ready quite
yet. Won't be long though. And the biscuits won't be ready
for a while, neither." The man wiped his hands on his apron
and reached for a knife to slice the ham for Longarm.

"We seen you go over to talk to those sons o' bitches
yesterday," the gentleman said over his shoulder as he
worked. "Did you do any good? Did you tell them they got
to move?" He sliced off a thick ham steak, complete with a
rim of juicy fat, and slapped it into a skillet. The skillet went
onto the stove. He opened the firebox and tossed in several
chunks of dried cow shit. Longarm might have preferred
that he at least wipe his hands again afterward, but a man
can't have everything.

The cook scrubbed some potatoes and began slicing
them, skin on. When he had what looked like a good pound
of the spuds he dropped those and a large dollop of lard into
another skillet and set that one beside the first.

Longarm relaxed, smoking a cheroot, and idly watched
the cook at his work.

His leisurely morning came to an abrupt halt when a bullet flew through the open doorway to thump into the back
wall of the café.

Longarm threw himself down, Colt in hand.

The cook looked around, annoyed but upright. "Oh, don't be worried, Marshal. That's probably some drunk cowboy from over Nebraska way. He's likely pissed off 'cause he knows you're about to close Stonecipher down and make those sons o' bitches all move someplace else. I wouldn't worry about it overmuch." He used a spatula to stir the potatoes and flip the ham over onto the other side. "Coffee should be ready soon," he said.

By then Longarm was already out the door, moving at a crouch in the dim predawn light.

Chapter 20

Nothing. He could see little and what he could see did not include any humans who might have fired that bullet.

Was the damn thing an attempt on his life? Or merely a warning? And if a warning or an assassination attempt, either one, the question remained: Why?

He was here trying to do good, trying to comply with a request for assistance. Whose ox was that goading and what were they doing that they would feel threatened by a U.S. deputy marshal's presence?

Unable to spot any idiot out for a morning stroll with a gun in hand, Longarm shoved his own .45 back into the leather and returned to the café.

"Coffee's ready," the cook said, stirring the skillet full of sliced potatoes.

"An' I'm ready for it," Longarm told him.

"If'n I was you," the man said, "I wouldn't worry about that stray gunshot. The cowboys come to town, they can get a mite rambunctious. You got to understand, Marshal, Valmere is the only town within a two-day ride, so when those boys have a few hours to get away from their work, they come here for whatever kind of blowout they're looking for. Mostly the want to get liquored up and then get laid." He looked over his shoulder and smiled. "Come morning they got to scramble to get back to the ranch and go to work again. My guess would be that shot came from the back of a cow pony on its way back home. The cowboy on top of that horse likely was just making some last-minute fireworks. I wouldn't think anything about it, was I you."

"Thanks for the advice. About that coffee . . . ?"

"I'm not forgetting you. Just don't want your breakfast to burn. Here you go." The cook laid down his spatula and plucked a coffee cup off a pile of them stacked on a shelf. He filled the cup and set it in front of Longarm, then added a bowl of sugar and a freshly opened can of condensed milk. "Let me get you a spoon."

The coffee was fresh if not overly strong. If nothing else, it washed some of the fur off Longarm's tongue. And the ham and fried spuds that followed filled the empty void in his belly.

He just wished he knew if the cook was right about that gunshot.

Longarm grunted softly, then tried to put the incident out of mind while he concentrated on surrounding that good breakfast.

Chapter 21

Longarm was not entirely sure just how a town marshal should act. And he was there as a substitute for a town marshal. That sort of thing was really not heavy in his experience. Enforcing the local laws would be the biggest part of it, he assumed, but in this case he did not know what the local laws were. Or even if there were any.

Just keeping order should do it, he decided. With that in mind, after breakfast he got out onto the sidewalk fronting the main street and made a show of his presence.

He ambled back and forth. Walked down to the livery and checked on his horse. Stopped in at the mercantile and bought some cigars. Dropped by the saloon for a brief chat with the bartender. Had a cup of coffee at the café.

Then he went across to the Nebraska side and did the same thing over there.

And received the same comments when he chatted with the residents.

"Are you gonna make those people go the hell away and leave us alone?"

"Say, Marshal, how long before those people have to move out?"

"Have you given them a deadline, Marshal?"

"When will it be, Marshal?"

Longarm would have found it almost funny, both sides saying the exact same things. Except they were serious, and there was the strong possibility of a war breaking out here.

Which was probably why someone, some soul with a clearer head on his shoulders, put together this request for the assistance of a federal deputy.

Everyone knew about the request and now about the presence of the deputy they had asked for. Yet no one seemed to know exactly who proposed the idea and sent for help. He wished now that he had looked at the message Billy Vail received requesting that help, but he had not thought it important at the time and now it was too late.

There was not even a telegraph line connecting Valmere and Stonecipher—or Valstone if one preferred—to the rest of the world, so he could not use that method to ask Billy about the signature on the request. If there was one and if the signature was real or simply a fabrication that someone made up to get him there.

For good or for ill, then, he was on his own here and would remain that way until he worked this out.

If he worked the towns' problems out. That was a very big "if," considering that neither side seemed to want to work it out. They just wanted the other side gone.

And after that random bullet into the café this morning, it was possible that someone—someone on either side of the divide—wanted him gone as well.

There were times when he wished he had stayed back in West by-God Virginia and spent his days staring at the ass end of a mule and walking along behind a plow.

Chapter 22

"Fight! There's a fight behind the livery." The cry rang out in the street. Longarm threw down the stub of the cigar he had been smoking and broke into a run toward the livery. A dozen men up and down the street ran with him.

He burst into the livery barn and ran on through to the corrals in back where he could hear shouts of encouragement.

When he got there he discovered at least a score of men already perched on the top rails of one of the smaller corrals, lined up there like so many birds decorating a telegraph wire.

Inside the enclosure there were two men, both liberally decorated in dust and blood. The two circled each other slowly, each crouching and with fists upraised.

"All right, damnit, break this up," Longarm barked.

No one paid the least bit of attention to him, so he repeated the demand. And once more. Finally one of the spectators turned and informed him, "These boys been working up to this for a month, Marshal. Time they work it out betwixt themselves."

"I thought Wyoming boys and Nebraska hands didn't mix none," Longarm said.

The cowboy who had spoken gave Longarm an odd look and said, "Hell, Marshal, these is both Wyoming boys, Dave there works for the MCX and Charley is a XL Bar rider. But Dave, he used to ride XL Bar, too. That's where them two got crossways. They just don't like each other." The fellow spoke while looking over his shoulder at the two combatants. He winced as one of the men landed a solid left hook that split the cheek of the other man and brought even more blood.

"They came back here deliberate?" Longarm asked. But by then he was talking to the backs of the crowd atop the fence. No one was paying attention to him.

Since this was what might be considered a "friendly" fight, Longarm exercised a little discretion. He crawled up onto an empty bit of fence rail and he, too, watched the fight progress below him.

Longarm had no idea which man was Dave and which was Charley, but it was clear that neither one was an accomplished fighter. For the most part they were more enthusiastic than effective. They threw roundhouse punches that rarely connected. Grappled often. Grunted and swore. And hit hard as hell on the rare occasion when one of their punches did land.

They reminded Longarm of a pair of aging bulls, bellowing and snorting and throwing dust but not actually doing much damage. What the hell, he thought. Let the two of them work this out. He saw no need for the law to intervene.

Dave and Charley were quickly wearing down, he saw. They were both gasping for air. One of them, the taller of the two, went to his knees. The other instead of taking advantage of his opponent's distress himself moved back and grabbed at a fence rail for support while he tried to get his breath. After a few moments the tall one stumbled to his feet and, fists inexpertly raised, the slow circling resumed.

More and more spectators rushed to the scene, shouting and jostling and taking bets on the outcome of the fight.

At least two more fights broke out but were briefly quelled, if only because those belligerents also wanted to witness the long-anticipated meeting between Dave, who represented the honor of the MCX, turned out to be the tall, lean redhead and Charley, from the XL Bar, who was the shorter, stocky fellow in the blood-soaked cavalry blouse.

Longarm rather enjoyed being a spectator himself for a change, especially since the two in the corral below were doing little real damage to one another.

If pressed, he would have to admit to doing a little shouting himself. Then it was over, both men staggering away to their own sides, each man assured by his companions that he had won.

And the two groups heading off in harmony to drink and recount the fight blow by blow—at least as they remembered it—in perfect harmony, everyone crowded into the same saloon, there being only the one on the Wyoming side of town. Or towns, plural, if one preferred.

Longarm took care to stay away from that saloon for the time being so all hands could work things out without the presence of the Law to interfere.

All in all, he thought, not a bad day, as he walked slowly across to the Nebraska side of things and the saloon on that side of town.

Chapter 23

"Getting much business, Marshal?" the barkeep asked.

"Not a lot. Which is just exactly the way I like it." Longarm finished his beer—infinitely better than the dishwater they served over in Wyoming—and wiped the suds off his mustache.

"Another?" the barman asked.

Longarm nodded. "You serve a good beer."

"Fresh," the barkeep said. "I have it freighted in every other week, rain or shine."

"What about snow?" Longarm asked.

"Now that can be a problem," the barman said. "But I stock up heavy each fall. Only had one winter bad enough that I ran out."

"How many winters have you been here?"

The barkeep laughed. "Two."

Longarm chuckled. And dipped his beak in that second, very fresh beer. He brought a cheroot out and used his teeth to nip the twist off, spat the twist into his palm, and stuck the cheroot between his teeth. "Match, please."

To deny a man, any man, the use of a match would have been a dire insult in any saloon. The barkeep quickly produced one and even struck it for Longarm.

"Thanks."

The barkeep grunted an acknowledgment and turned to his other customers. The place was not as busy as in the saloon over on the Wyoming side, but it was much quieter.

Longarm stood at the bar for a time, enjoying his beer and his smoke, then nodded a thank-you to the barkeep and ambled out into the evening.

It was about time he should be thinking about a bite of supper, and he thought perhaps Elizabeth Kunsler would like to share the meal with him. Accordingly he turned in that direction.

He was halfway there when he heard a loud commotion from across the way in Wyoming.

And soon on the heels of that disturbance heard the flat, dull reports of a pair of gunshots.

Longarm put aside his thoughts of dinner with Liz and headed at a dead run toward the Wyoming-side saloon.

Chapter 24

"Dead" run indeed.

When he got to the Wyoming-side saloon, Longarm found short, stocky Charley from the XL Bar laid out on the floor, his revolver beside him, and the tall redhead named Dave standing at the bar nearby.

Dave had his revolver in his holster, but it was obvious enough who had done the shooting here. No one wanted to stand close to Dave. The other patrons who had crowded into the place were managing to keep their distance despite the crowd.

Longarm stood for a moment, playing the sounds back in his head. He had heard two gunshots. Exactly two. Which meant it was entirely possible that this had been a fair fight, just like the fistfight between the two had been.

Before doing anything else he picked Charley's Smith & Wesson .44 Russian up off the floor. The S&Ws were break-top models. Longarm released the catch and flipped the cylinder up.

The pistol was loaded with six fat, stubby .44 cartridges. Fully loaded. None of the cartridges had been fired as he could easily see by glancing at the unblemished primers, but just to satisfy himself that he was not making a mistake he dropped all six into his palm, looked them over and returned them to the chambers.

He snapped the S&W closed and dropped the gun onto Charley's belly. Charley did not mind. The cowboy was beyond feeling anything. Ever. The man was dead as a shoat on a spit.

Longarm walked over and faced Dave.

"What's your name, mister?"

"Dave Ashford, Marshal, and this here was a fair fight."

"Was it?" Longarm's eyes were cold, hard, and unblinking. They bore twin holes into Ashford's suddenly sweating face.

"I, uh . . . 'course it was," Ashford said. He took his bandanna and wiped his forehead and cheeks with it.

"Give me your gun," Longarm ordered.

"Where I come from, Marshal, a man don't hand his gun over to somebody else," Ashford blustered.

"All right," Longarm said mildly. "If you'd rather I shoot you an' then look at it, you're entitled t' the difference."

Dave Ashford forked over his Colt, very careful to do it quietly, slowly, and with only two fingers lest this cold-eyed lawman mistake his movement for resistance. "Here y'go, Marshal, but I'm telling you, this here was a fair fight."

"Uh-huh." Longarm flipped open the loading gate on the Colt, drew the hammer back to half cock, and spun the cylinder. Two of the five cartridges had been fired.

"Ask anybody," Dave urged.

"I should maybe ask some of the MCX riders?" Longarm asked.

Dave motioned in a half circle around him. "These fellows is all witnesses to what happened. They'll tell you."

"I'm sure they will," Longarm said. He smiled although the expression did not reach his eyes. "I never yet met a man who wouldn't stand up for a bunkmate whether the son of a bitch . . . no implication 'bout you when I say that . . . whether the fellow was right or wrong."

Dave reached for his .45, but Longarm stuffed it into his waistband rather than hand it over just yet.

He looked around the room, then called out, "Anybody here who *isn't* from either the MCX or the XL Bar?"

"Me, sir," a sawed-off little runt of a man said, stepping out of the crowd to present himself in front of Longarm. "I'm drifting through. I don't work for nobody right now."

"Ever worked for either o' those brands?" Longarm asked.

"No, sir."

"Ever worked with any o' these men?"

The little fellow took a moment to look around, then shook his head.

"All right, tell me what happened here."

"This fella"—he pointed to Dave—"got to argiffying with that'un." This time he pointed down at the dead man. "That'un said something that I didn't hear, then that'un"—again he pointed at Dave—"drew down on t'other one and shot him dead. Shot him twice in the chest and belly. That'un managed to get his gun out but he never come close to getting off a shot."

"So this one"—Longarm pointed to Ashford—"drew first?"

The witness nodded. "Had his gun out and smoke in the air before that'un ever reached for his gun."

"Thanks." He motioned to George Griner, who was behind the bar. "This man drinks on me this evening."

"Whatever you say, Marshal."

Longarm did not ask Griner anything about the fight. Whatever the supposedly neutral bartender might say, he would risk alienating one group of cowboys or the other. Longarm would come back when the place was empty and ask Griner what he saw. But not now. He did not want to ruin the man's business.

Instead, Longarm turned to Dave Ashford and, expression now grim, said, "Turn around."

"But I tell you . . ."

"Turn the fuck around while you still can."

Ashford turned around. Quickly.

"Hands behind the back."

"But I can't . . ."

Longarm's Colt flashed, but instead of firing it, he used the butt to buffalo Dave Ashford, dropping the man to the floor where Longarm trussed him with his hands behind his back.

Longarm reached up to the bar and grabbed Ashford's beer then poured it onto his head. That brought Ashford around although he still looked more than a little woozy from the blow Longarm had given him.

"Now," Longarm said, looking around the suddenly not crowded room, "where's the jail around here?"

Chapter 25

"Jail? Marshal, we got no jail here. I mean, we never had a marshal here before now, neither, so we never had need for a jail," George Griner volunteered. He smiled, a rather apologetic expression, and spread his hands wide.

"What the hell do you do when you have a problem?" Longarm asked, incredulous.

"Why, if somebody acts up too bad we'd tell him he couldn't come back for a spell. We wouldn't let the guy come have a drink or visit the whorehouse or anything like that. He just pretty much couldn't come to town at all for a month, two months, whatever." Griner's smile flickered nervously on and off again.

"He couldn't just go over to the other side to drink in Nebraska instead?" Longarm asked.

"Well, you see, yeah. That was the problem."

"And so you sent for me?" Longarm guessed.

"Well, um . . . yeah." Griner set a mug in front of Longarm and said, "Can I get you a beer, Marshal? Or anything?"

Longarm shook his head. "No, thanks, but you can get me the town council, or whatever you call them here. I need t' have a word with whoever is in charge. In the meantime . . ." He looked around. "In the meantime I want t' borrow your stove."

Griner blinked. "Our stove?"

"Right. The one in the back o' the room there," Longarm said, pointing toward the cast-iron stove that had been shoved out of the way. It did not appear to be connected to any chimney or stovepipe, although there was a pie plate tacked to the wall that suggested it was where a stovepipe existed. Presumably the stove would be connected when fall weather brought cold temperatures.

"Sure, Marshal, whatever you want." The bartender laughed, thinking Longarm was making a joke although one he obviously did not understand.

Longarm tugged on Dave Ashford's arm. "Come along, mister." He took Ashford back to the stove and used a spare set of handcuffs looped around a leg of the stove to secure the prisoner there. The stove was a big one, intended to heat the entire saloon. Longarm guessed it would weigh four hundred pounds or more. Ashford was not going anywhere, at least not for the time being.

Leaving Ashford sitting on the floor beside the stove, Longarm returned to George Griner. "Clear the place out, George. Everyone out. Including the dead man there. Then I want you t' fetch your boss an' all the other bigwigs. Them an' me are gonna have us a talk."

Chapter 26

Longarm stood glaring at the civic leaders—such as they were—of Valmere, Wyoming Territory. His look reflected pure disgust. Hands on hips, he declared, "I cannot believe you fuckers have been so wrapped up in your fight with the folks across the street that you neglected even the most basic needs o' this here town. An' before you get all hot an' bothered, I'm gonna have this same talk with the people over in Nebraska.

"What I am gonna do right now is assess each an' every one of you ten dollars. It'll be used for civic improvement, by the way. I'm not gonna take any of it. My salary is paid by the fed'ral government, so don't get to thinking any o' that shit. But there are things that have t' be bought.

"Now where is the nearest telegraph office? Somebody speak up. Anybody."

"Lusk or Torrington, one of them," Otis Reed piped up.

"Fine. Thank you. Who has a fast horse and a couple days to spend helping out." He waited. After a moment he said, "Don't everybody speak up at once here."

No one did.

Longarm waited another minute or so, then said, "Hettie, you have a handyman at your place, I assume."

The plump little black madam nodded. "I do."

"I want to borrow him for a couple days then."

The woman nodded again. "His name is Benjamin. He's a good man."

Longarm pulled a sheet of paper from his coat pocket. "Give this to Benjamin. He can use my horse. Oh, and give him this dollar. He's to go t' town an' send this wire off. The address is wrote down there."

"What are . . . ?"

"It's an order for certain materials. Meantime, Jamison, you have a heavy wagon, don't you?"

The owner of the mercantile nodded.

"I want you t' send a work crew over to Hat Creek. There's timber there. Sure as hell ain't none around here, so go where they can find it. I want logs, something stout an' straight that can be shaped into puncheons for flooring. Each one has t' cut to at least ten feet. Longer would be even better. Make sure you send someone with some sense. An' some tools. An' some grub for 'bout a week."

"How's come we have to supply everything, Marshal? What about those bastards over there?" Jacob Potts gestured angrily toward the Stonecipher side of the twin towns.

"Believe me, they are gonna contribute their full share, an' they are gonna pay their assessments, too. You both are, so get used t' that idea. On this deal, you are working together."

"What are we working together for?" a voice in the back called. Longarm could not see who asked the question.

"What we are doing," Longarm said, "is building a jail. An' by the way, I've seen a lot o' odd pieces o' lumber laying around behind your store buildings. You might 's well know, I'm confiscating all of it. That's what we'll use for the walls an' whatnot."

"You can't have a jail without a cell," the same voice said.

"That's what's in the telegram I just gave to Hettie to send. It's an order for a prefabricated jail cell. Outfit over in Omaha sells them. Also metal roofing. Shit like that. Should

be pretty much everything we need. I assume you have nails
an' hammers an' like that over to the general store, but I'm
sending off for the major items."

"That's what the assessment is for?"

Longarm nodded. "'Tis."

"Which side are you going to build this jail of yours,
Marshal?"

He grinned and reached for a cheroot. "Neither. It's
gonna go right smack in the middle. Now if you fellas will
excuse me, all this talk has got me thirsty. George, start
pouring. An' everybody . . . leave your money on the bar
there so's we can pay for all this civic improvement."

Chapter 27

"I swear, Custis dear, you're so busy these days that I hardly ever get to see you. Won't you come have supper with me tonight?" Liz trailed her fingernails lightly across the back of his neck, sending a chill down Longarm's spine.

He grinned. "Just supper?"

"Mmm, could be more."

"I'll find the time. But if I'm a little late, don't give up on me. I'll get there just as soon as I can."

"If you want, you can bring your things and stay there with me. I don't know why you insist on staying over there with those whores."

"'Cause for one thing, I don't wanta compromise you. After all, I won't be here forever, and you have to live with these people after I'm gone." He laughed. "Besides, those whores have kinda adopted me for a pet or something. They can't figure out why I'm not fucking any of 'em."

"You really aren't?" Liz asked.

"No, I'm really not. Now go start fixing a fancy supper or whatever 'tis you ladies do in the afternoons. I got t' see to the building of my jail. The cell pieces arrived an' I need to get Otis to put it together. Either him or the Stonecipher blacksmith. What's his name? Oh, right. Adam. Anyhow, they got forges, so they're the ones can put it together. Then once they do that, the carpenters can finish that last wall."

Elizabeth just shook her head. And walked away. "I'll see you this evening, Custis."

"Right. Thanks," he said absently, his mind already elsewhere.

Chapter 28

Longarm worked with the volunteers—he knew they were volunteers because he had volunteered them himself—until dusk put an end to the day.

"Reckon it's time," he called, "but we did good today."

He stepped back and looked at what they had accomplished so far. The floor was down—good, heavy puncheons that would be almost impossible for a prisoner to dig through—and the framing was complete. Two walls were up and a good start had been made on the third.

They could not build the fourth wall until the Nebraska side's wagon returned from the railroad at Kimball. The wagon would be carrying the prefabricated cell sections, and those would not fit inside if the walls were complete. The same wagon should have the sheet metal roof sections. As it was now the rafters were in place, but the roofing material had not yet arrived.

"She's looking good, Long," one of the workmen called.

"Thanks to you and the other fellows, Harry," Longarm responded. "Good night, now. Good night all."

He walked over to Hettie's whorehouse and went in without knocking. Except for being a mite noisy at night the whorehouse was as good as most hotels and better than some.

He waved to the girls sitting in the parlor waiting for customers. There were two of them at the moment, which meant the other three were upstairs draining the sap out of some cowboys.

Longarm went upstairs, stripped off his shirt and washed, then changed to a clean shirt and buckled his gun belt back in place. He pulled on his vest and coat, then grabbed his Stetson and headed back down the stairs.

"Going out for dinner tonight?" Hettie asked when he reached the front hall.

"Yes'm."

The madam laughed. "My girls will be disappointed. They like it when you're here. I think every one of them is in love with you or has convinced herself that she is. You, uh, you do know that you wouldn't have to pay to have one of them, don't you? Any one of them."

Longarm leaned down and kissed the top of Hettie's head. "I know." He laughed. "But how could I possibly choose just one when they are all so lovely?" That was something of an exaggeration. Hettie's girls were of average appearance at best. He had no idea how any of them were as to performance.

Longarm paused before stepping into the vestibule. "Can I ask you 'bout something that's been vexing me?"

"Of course. Anything."

"Why is this place called Stella's when I've never met anybody here by that name?"

"Can you keep a secret, Marshal?"

"Ayuh, I can do that."

"Stella's is owned by me and by a partner. We made the name what we did because each of us has a reason we don't want to be known as an owner. Me because I'm not sure menfolk would want to come to a cathouse that's owned by a nigger woman, my partner because he don't want his name associated with a whorehouse. So we picked a name out of a hat, so to speak, and called it Stella's. But there isn't no Stella, at least not here."

Longarm laughed. "It makes sense when you tell it that way. All right then, Hettie, thanks. I'll, uh, I might be late tonight."

"That's all right. We be open whenever you get here."

"Yes, I expect you will at that." He stepped out onto the porch.

Off in the distance there was a flash of light. A moment later a heavy bullet slammed into one of the uprights that held the porch roof up.

Chapter 29

Longarm hit the ground, .45 in hand, searching for a glimpse of form or motion out where he had seen the muzzle flash. He knew good and well that the distance was too long for a revolver. It would take a rifle to make the shot. But he was more than willing to try it if only he had something to shoot at, damnit.

One thing he knew for certain. That shot had come from the Nebraska side of things. Someone over there wanted him dead or otherwise gone.

He lay on the ground outside the nonexistent Stella's whorehouse for a good half hour, until he heard some revelers loudly and drunkenly approaching. Then he stood and brushed himself off, slid the Colt back into his leather and shivered. Although the evening air was far from being cold.

He stopped by the smithy, where Otis was keeping an eye on Dave Ashford. The prisoner was shackled to the larger of Otis's anvils. Longarm figured if the man could make a run for freedom with that monster under his arm, then he was entitled to get away.

"Cocksucker," Ashford snarled when Longarm walked in. Then the man looked away, unwilling to meet Longarm's eye.

"I see our boy is in his normal good humor," Longarm said.

Otis Reed chuckled and gave his bellows a couple of tugs, then used a pair of long tongs to adjust some bits of iron half buried in white-hot coke. "It's a pity I can't put him to use around here," he said, "but he won't do shit, just sits there and glares at anyone who comes near. His curiosity value has worn out. I think now he's keeping customers away."

"Do you want me to move him?" Longarm asked.

"No, but I hope the circuit judge comes around soon. You did send for him, didn't you?"

Longarm nodded. "Just like the council authorized me to."

"Any idea when the man will get here?"

Longarm bit the twist off a cheroot and used Otis's tongs to pick up a cherry-red piece of coke. He used that to light his smoke before he answered. "There's no telling about those fellows. They travel when they can, where they have to. Have you ever had a proper judge come through Valmere?"

"There hasn't been one since I've been here," Reed said, "and I got here within a few months of the first buildings to go up." He grunted and retrieved the tongs from Longarm so he could turn the pieces of iron again. "Of course back then we thought the whole shebang was in Wyoming. That was before the government surveyor came through and screwed everything up."

"Government will do that, y'know," Longarm said. "Sometimes I think that's what it does best."

"Yet you work for the government," Reed said.

"To that, sir, I plead guilty." He took another pull on his cheroot and slowly blew the smoke out, then said, "Time for me t' head for supper. What with building that jail, swinging a hammer an' all I've worked up an appetite. First actual work I've done in, I dunno, in years."

"Well, you needn't worry about your prisoner. I'll take good care of the son of a bitch," Reed said.

Ashford swung his head around and glared at them. "Fuck the both of you."

Longarm ignored the man, said good night to Otis, and walked across the wide street, past the partially finished jail to Liz Kunsler's modest house. When he mounted her front porch he could smell what promised to be a fine supper.

And after that, well, he was looking forward to afterward even more than to the meal.

Chapter 30

"That was a mighty fine meal," Longarm said, dropping his napkin onto the table and pushing his chair back. He grinned. "Now for dessert."

Liz's brow wrinkled in consternation. "Custis, I didn't make any dessert."

He laughed. "Honey, you *are* the dessert."

"Well, in that case," she said, rising from the table and coming into his arms.

"You taste like mashed potatoes an' gravy," he mumbled into her mouth moments later.

Liz pulled her face away. "What a terrible thing to say!"

"Darlin'," he said with a laugh. "I happen t' *like* mashed potatoes an' gravy."

"Then perhaps you should see what other flavors you can find," she said.

"Fine by me. Let me look." He kissed her some more, then suggested, "Think maybe we could move this back to your bedroom so's I can look closer? An' in other places?"

"I think we could arrange that." Liz stepped back and took his hand, leading him back to the bedroom. She lighted a lamp there and turned the wick down to a soft glow. But bright enough that he could see—and admire—her body as the lady stepped out of her dress.

"I think I'm getting ahead of you here," she said, breaking his concentration on what he was so thoroughly enjoying seeing. Longarm quickly began shedding clothing in an effort to catch up.

They came together then, naked and eager. He could feel his cock pressed between their bellies. Could feel the sharp jut of her hip bones and the softness of her tits against his chest. Could feel the desire in her mouth.

Liz smiled when he picked her up and placed her gently onto the bed. "Fuck me," she whispered into his mouth.

He kissed his way down. Her mouth. Her throat. Her chest. Each rigid nipple in turn. Lower, across her belly and into the tangled bush. He found the sweet nectar in her pussy and licked the tiny button of her pleasure until Liz cried out in a powerful orgasm.

By then she was clawing at him. Wanting him. Insisting that their bodies be joined.

She twisted around so that they lay with their heads at the foot of the bed, but Liz did not want to wait long enough to change. She groped at his cock. Took it in her fist and pulled him to her. Into her.

Longarm plunged into the wet depths of Elizabeth's body, immersing himself in her, surrounding himself with her heat.

She was able to accommodate all of him and he thrust deep. He lifted her knees and draped them over his shoulders so her ass was high off the bed. He took hold of her tits and rammed full length into her. He could feel the head of his cock bump into something inside her. For a moment he worried that he might hurt her, but he had gone beyond being able to stop. He thrust deep, over and over and over again. He could feel his sap rising. Could feel the sweet gathering of pressure deep inside his balls.

And then it exploded. His come spewed out into her, and he let out a loud grunt as the pleasure overwhelmed him.

Liz came again at the same moment. She clutched him tight and drummed her heels against the small of his back in an attempt to pull him even deeper.

Finally he went limp. He allowed Liz's legs to fall away from his shoulders, and she lay exhausted on the bed. Longarm let his weight down onto her, and she hugged him close.

They dropped off to sleep like that.

Chapter 31

Longarm woke . . . he had no idea what the time might be, only knew it was late. And he was satiated after his tryst with Liz, happily satiated. He slipped out of bed without waking her, found his clothes, and got dressed in the dim light of her bedside lamp.

Once he was fully dressed he leaned down and delivered a light kiss to Liz's cheek, then blew out the lamp and felt his way through the dark house to the front door.

He let himself out but did not immediately leave. Instead he sat in one of the rocking chairs on Liz's porch and lighted a cheroot. He sat there for a little while enjoying the soft, evening air and the coolness of the night.

He could hear the sounds of revelry from the two whorehouses, one here on the Nebraska side, the other from Stella's on the Wyoming side of town.

Town, he reflected. That right there was the problem. The people here persisted in thinking of this as being two separate towns when by all rights it was, or should be, a single community.

And Custis Long was acting town marshal for both sides, enforcing the laws of Wyoming Territory and of the state of

Nebraska. Worse, the divided community had no town laws of its own. None.

It was a wonder, he thought, that the cowboys from nearby outfits hadn't been riding roughshod over the whole shebang.

He sat, rocking back and forth and thinking, until he finished his cigar. Then he flipped the butt into the darkness. It hit the ground in a cascade of flying sparks.

Longarm stood, paused for another quiet moment to enjoy the night, then stepped down off Liz's porch and walked across the wide street to Stella's whorehouse and the comfort of his bed.

Chapter 32

"Good morning, Marshal."

"Good morning, Otis."

"What can I do for you, Marshal?"

"I just came t' get my horse."

"Lordy, you aren't leaving us, are you?"

"No, Otis. Just taking a ride."

"Oh. Right. Let me get that horse for you, marshal. You just set and relax. I'll saddle him and fetch him to you."

"That's mighty nice o' you, Otis."

"Happy to oblige, Marshal."

Ten minutes later Longarm was heading at an easy jog north of town. The day was a pleasant one with a few puffy clouds floating overhead and the sound of songbirds trilling in the brush he passed through.

He was comfortable, a hot breakfast behind his belt and the sun warm on his face. The gray horse moved at an easy pace. It seemed a shame that all days could not be like this.

He almost regretted arriving at his destination. It took only a scant few minutes to reach the water that was responsible for the presence of both Valmere and Stonecipher. Surprising, too.

Longarm was expecting to see a pond. This was a small

lake, covering probably eight or ten acres and rimmed with cattails. He had no idea how deep the water might be, but it was obvious there was plenty of it even if it turned out to be shallow water.

He stepped down off the gray and squatted on the top of a low rise to light a cheroot and enjoy the feel of the day.

While he watched, a wagon approached pulled by a pair of cobs and carrying four barrels. The driver carefully backed his outfit down to the water's edge, then climbed down and used a bucket to begin filling the barrels.

It was a slow and cumbersome process but the burly fellow—Longarm was sure he had seen the man in town on the Nebraska side—seemed to know what he was doing and went at it with dogged determination.

After several minutes Longarm mounted the gray and rode down to the lakeside where the gent continued to work at filling his barrels.

"Mornin'." Longarm touched the brim of his Stetson.

"Good morning yourself." The man with the bucket continued to work at his task.

"Could I ask what you're doing?" Longarm said.

The fellow gave him a look that was just short of disgust. "Filling these barrels, of course." His tone of voice suggested that Longarm must be daft if he could not see what he was doing.

Longarm smiled. "No, sir, I mean *why* are you doin' this hard work."

"Everybody needs water, mister. To drink, to wash with, whatever, everybody needs water one way or another. I sell it to them. Wallace Waterman, they call me. That ain't my right name, but it's what everybody calls me. And you would be that marshal from down Denver way, name of Long." He nodded as if affirming his own statement but continued to dip his bucket into the edge of the lake and empty it into one of his barrels.

"How long does it take you to fill all four of those barrels?" Longarm asked.

"Oh, couple hours, I suppose. I can make two, sometimes three trips out here each day. Only one on Sundays. Sunday mornings I rest. Sundays the folks in town have to use less water."

"Can't they come get it for themselves?"

Wallace the Water Man grinned. "They ain't allowed to."

"How's that?" Longarm asked.

"'Cause I filed on this land. Own it legal and clear. Or anyhow will once I've been on it long enough to prove up."

"Wise," Longarm commented.

"I ain't no scholar," Wallace said, "but I ain't maybe as dumb as I look." With pride in his voice he added, "I can read and cipher, you know." He splashed another bucket of lake water into a barrel.

"Thanks for the information, Wallace. Mind if I water my horse here?"

"That will be all right if he bends down and drinks, him or you either one, but you can't lift it up to him. That's the law. Water rights. I know about them," Wallace said proudly. "I read all about it in one of those gummint brochures."

"Right you are," Longarm said. He led the gray to the edge of the lake, but the horse had no interest in drinking at the moment. "Thank you again, sir." He stepped onto the horse, nodded good-bye to Wallace Waterman, and reined the gray back toward the twin towns.

It was time for him to get back to the nearly complete jail. And to see that Dave Ashford was fed and had a trip to the outhouse.

Chapter 33

Longarm had to keep everything in balance. Two carpenters from Valmere; two carpenters from Stonecipher. One man with pick and shovel from Wyoming; one man with pick and shovel from Nebraska. And never mind that only one man at a time could work in the hole that would serve as the latrine. Balance between the twin towns, always balance.

"When you're finished putting that last wall in place," he told them, "start on the outhouse. An' after that, build me some stools, a cot for inside the cell, stuff like that. We can't afford t' buy ready-made furniture so's we'll just build what we need. Oh, an' make me a desk, too, please. An' some shelves to go on that wall there. I'll need someplace t' file the records." He sighed. "Two pairs o' shelves, I suppose, since the records will have t' be kept separate for the two towns."

"That will keep us busy another two, maybe three days," carpenter Tom Faroe said.

"Whatever it takes," Longarm told the man. Faroe was a good worker, sent by Cal Bonham, the Stonecipher storekeeper; Longarm liked Faroe. Liked Bonham too for that matter.

"Are you leaving already, Marshal?"

"Just t' see to my prisoner. I figure to take him for lunch,

then back here so's he can have the honor of bein' the first
prisoner in that brand-new jail cell. For a few days anyhow
till the Wyoming circuit judge gets here. Then I s'pose you
boys will have to come back an' build us a gallows."

"Whatever you say, Marshal," Faroe said.

Longarm headed across the wide street to Garrett Franz's
general mercantile, where Dave Ashford was chained to
a post. When he got there the prisoner was curled up into a
tight ball, lying with his back to the store.

"Wake up, Ashford. It's time I can take you for a shit an'
a wash and something to eat. Personally I'm hungry, so rattle
your bones an' get around, man."

Ashford did not move. Longarm nudged him in the butt
with the toe of his boot. Still the man did not so much as
quiver.

"Uh-oh!" Longarm knelt behind the man, wary lest Ashford
was trying to pull a fast one and make a break for freedom.

Dave Ashford was already free. Free from bondage, free
from pain, free from life.

"Well, shit," Longarm said, rising to his feet. He removed
his Stetson and wiped his forehead.

He turned to Franz and asked, "Is there a doctor here-
abouts?"

"Over in Lusk there's a pretty good man. I don't know
as he'd be willing to come here, but we've sent a few of our
really sick folks over to him. The drive only takes a day and
a half," Franz said.

"We're not gonna go t' all that trouble," Longarm said.
He knelt again, rolled Ashford onto his back, and began
unbuttoning the man's shirt.

Chapter 34

There was a small, a very small, puncture wound high in the man's belly, just below his rib cage. Apparently someone had stuck Ashford with . . . Longarm did not know what sort of implement might have been used. An ice pick probably or at least something very similar.

The general store was full of utilitarian objects that could have been used, or the killer could have brought his own.

When one got right down to it, Longarm thought, it did not all that much matter what had been used to kill David Ashford. The question that mattered was *why?*

Longarm stood and rolled Ashford back onto his side, facing away from the store as he had been when Longarm got there. He walked to the front of the place, where Garrett Franz was waiting on a customer, a woman Longarm recognized as being the wife of one of the townsfolk.

When the lady had made her purchases as left, Longarm approached Franz.

"I need t' ask you a few things, Garrett," he said.

"Of course, Marshal. What can I do for you?"

"It's about the prisoner there. Has he been arguin' with anybody?"

"Not that I saw. In fact he has been very quiet this morning. Why?"

"The reason the man's been quiet, Garrett, is 'cause he's dead," Longarm said, reaching for a cheroot.

"Dead! My God! How? Why?" Franz blurted.

"I was thinkin' you might have some answers to them very questions," Longarm said, flicking a match aflame with his thumbnail and using it to light his cigar. "The man was right there in plain sight, after all. In your store. Practically under your nose. You must've saw something, heard something." He blew a cloud of pale smoke between them. "So what is it that you know about this?"

"Nothing. I swear to you, I neither saw nor heard anything out of the ordinary this morning. The prisoner has been . . . that is, I thought he was sleeping late this morning. I didn't want to disturb him."

"And last night?"

"The store was busy last night. You yourself gave him supper. After he ate it I collected the empty dishes and took them over to the café where they belonged. That part was later, of course. I got busy with waiting on customers and didn't really pay any attention to Ashford. Didn't see or hear anything out of the ordinary. Not that I can recall."

"There was no fight? No hot words or low whispering with someone?" Longarm asked.

"No, not that I noticed. But to tell you the truth, my hearing is not everything it used to be. It helps if I can watch a man's lips move. The way I'm doing with you right now. But sounds behind my back . . ." Franz shrugged. "They would have to be loud. Last night I heard nothing."

Longarm grunted. He was not satisfied, certainly was not happy with the storekeeper's responses. But then if the man had heard nothing . . . or would not admit to anything . . . there was little that Longarm could do about it.

"All right. Thanks." Longarm turned and started out.

"Wait," Franz called.

Longarm stopped. Turned back to face the man. "Yes?"

"The, um, the body. You can't just leave a dead person on my floor there."

"My advice," Longarm said, "would be t' have him removed an' buried wherever you do such of a thing around here." He gave Franz a solemn nod. "But you do whatever 'tis you think best."

Then he turned and proceeded out of the store to the street beyond.

Chapter 35

Late that morning the two men with the picks and shovels came to him. "Marshal, unless you want us to dig until we come out the other side, I think your shit pit is done. You want to come take a look?"

He did. The sump was a good eight or nine feet down and plenty wide. The soil underground looked like it would provide more than adequate drainage for the liquids. Longarm nodded his satisfaction.

"Thanks for your help, fellas. You can go back to your regular jobs now."

"You don't need us swinging a hammer?" the Nebraska man offered.

"No, I think things are pretty much under control now. We have two working on the outhouse an' two making furniture. Things are lookin' good here, so go on an' thank you."

The pick and shovel brigade went back to their respective sides of the twin towns. Longarm turned to the other four and told them to take their lunch break. When they did, he noticed, they took their lunch pails and sat well apart from each other. He had been hoping that the work, of necessity in close quarters, would have led to something approaching friendship. It had not. He regretted the lack of camaraderie among them but knew there was no way to force it.

"If you need me, I'm gonna go have me something to eat, too. I'll be at McPhail's Café over yonder."

"You go ahead, Marshal," one of the Wyoming boys said.

Longarm walked across the wide street to Harrison McPhail's café on the Nebraska side for a quick lunch, then went back across to the Wyoming side for a drink in Jacob Potts's saloon. He was trying to show impartiality in his movements.

"My Lord, Jake, is this horse piss the best you have?" He had forgotten how very bad Potts's whiskey was.

Potts wiped an imaginary spot off the bar and grunted. "It's what there is, Long. Sorry if you don't like it, but you take it or leave it. It don't make no nevermind to me. The cowboys around here will drink what I give them or go thirsty. So will you."

"Except I can walk across the street there and get something decent in your brother's place. They could, too, if they wanted to."

"That man is no brother to me. He's just like all the rest of those sons o' bitches over there, and all the hands around here know it. We don't like those people any more than they like us, and one of these days we'll have us a showdown. Then there won't be but one town here, and it'll be a Wyoming town."

Longarm set his whiskey glass down, the contents barely tasted. The stuff really was terrible and he remembered now that the beer was just as bad. Either one left an unpleasant aftertaste in his mouth. He lighted a cheroot, thinking perhaps the flavor of the smoke would take away the taste of the whiskey. It did not, not completely, but it helped.

"I guess you heard, that MCX rider got himself murdered last night."

"I heard. Do you figure one of the XL Bar boys slipped

in and got some payback for him killing their pard Charley?"

"It's a possibility," Longarm admitted.

"Likely," Potts said, rubbing at his bartop some more. Longarm got the impression the man would rather talk about almost anything other than the quality of his drinks. Or talk about nothing at all, which appeared to be an even more attractive possibility to the man.

He thought about walking back to the whorehouse where Hettie said she had a decent bottle of whiskey but decided he really should get back to work instead. There were still the desk and shelving to be built and he wanted to make sure they were constructed to his satisfaction.

"Thanks for the drink," he told Potts.

"Anytime, Marshal. We all want to help any way we can."

Longarm gave the man a halfhearted wave and went back out into the glare of the midday sun.

Chapter 36

The town marshal's office was almost complete. The shelves were up and the carpenters were busy building a desk and stools. Longarm left them to their work and went first to Cal Bonham on the Nebraska side and then to Garrett Franz in Wyoming, collecting—or begging for—paper, ink, pens, and the like.

"I'm impressed," Bonham said. "You're bringing things together better than I ever thought you could."

"If you didn't think I could do much good here, why'd you send for me?" Longarm asked.

Bonham blinked. "Why, I . . . I didn't do that. Didn't have any part in having it done, either, Marshal."

"Then who did?" He still wished he had gotten a look at the signature on that wire asking Billy to render assistance to the local law.

Bonham shrugged. "Damn if I know, Marshal."

"That's interestin'. Say, you wouldn't have any o' them pushpin things, would you? Thumbtacks, I think they're called."

"I think I have some. Hold on. I'll see if I can find them," the Nebraska storekeeper said.

Across the wide street—and Nebraska state line—he posed the same question to the Wyoming storekeeper.

"No, I didn't send it," Franz responded. "I don't think any of our people did."

"But you knew about it. When I got here everyone was expecting me. Everyone on both sides, in fact."

Franz peered toward the ceiling and scratched his neck. He needed a shave. After a moment he said, "No," drawing the sound out a bit. "But I can't remember how I came to know you would be coming. Or one of your people, that is, not you in particular."

"Isn't that strange," Longarm mused. "No one admits to sending the wire. Or the letter or whatever the hell it was. Come t' think of it, Billy never showed me the actual paper. Could've been a wire. Could've been a letter. You do send mail from here, don't you?"

"Of course we do. I have a postal window in the back there. The wagon goes over to the highway once a week, every week, winter or summer. And let me tell you, getting anything through in the winter around here can be rugged."

"I'd think so," Longarm said. "Do you remember anybody sending a letter to the United States marshal down in Denver? Would've been a month, two months ago?"

"No, but then I don't have to look at the mail or sort it or anything. We don't have local service. The town is so small there's no need to buy a stamp to send a note to the next block over. Everything that's mailed from here is going somewhere else, so I bag it all up and send it down to Cheyenne. Incoming mail is another matter, of course. I sort that and hand it to the person the next time I see them."

"No boxes here," Longarm said.

"No, just the mail drop for outgoing mail and some pigeon holes in the back to hold mail until I see the recipient," Franz said.

Longarm grunted, lost for a moment in thought. Then he walked back across the street to Bonham's store and inquired of him about how he handled mail. He got essentially the same information from the Nebraska storekeeper.

"This is a contract station," Bonham said. "We sell a few stamps and handle mail going out or coming in. I send the outbound mail in a pouch that goes down to Kimball and the rail line."

"And the telegraph?"

"The nearest wires would be at Lusk, though we hope to get our own someday," Bonham told him.

"Damnit, Cal, some-damn-body represented himself as the town. Or towns. And asked for help from a whole company of deputies."

Bonham smiled. "So you are an entire company all by yourself?"

Longarm laughed. "That's me, all right."

The storekeeper became serious again when he said, "I wish I could help you, Marshal. I really do, but I don't know anything that would help. I didn't send any letter and I don't know who did."

"Yet everybody over on this side knew I was coming, just like across the way there," Longarm said. "It's odd. Damned odd."

"If you figure it out, let me know."

"Yeah, I'd be glad t' know that my own self. Oh, well. Say, d'you have any reasonably fresh cheroots? I could use some o' them things. Or a plain old rum crook if you don't have cheroots."

Chapter 37

Longarm lay propped up on two pillows, a heavy glass ashtray resting on his chest and a cheroot between his lips. Liz lay tucked in close beside him. Both were naked. Her right tit was pressing against the side of his chest.

"Ouch, damnit!" Longarm jumped, coming upright almost into a sitting position. Liz jumped, too. After a moment he grumbled a bit, then laughed.

"What was that all about? What did you do, honey?" Liz asked.

"I missed the damn ashtray, that's what I done. I like t' set my chest hair on fire with a chunk o' hot ash," he said.

He glanced down in time to see Liz's face contort in an effort to keep from laughing at his plight.

"Oh, you think that's funny, do you?"

"Well, now that you mention it," she said, "yes. It is."

"Why, you sorry little minx."

She gave up trying to hold it in and burst out laughing. A moment later Longarm began laughing too, laughter being a contagious sort of thing.

Once their laughter subsided he set the ashtray aside and—carefully—the cigar, too. Then he rolled onto his side, wrapped his arms around Elizabeth, and spent some time kissing her.

He ran his hand over her hip and up the indent of her waist, on to the soft fullness of her breast. When he began lightly rolling her nipple between his thumb and forefinger, Liz whispered into his mouth, "Oh, I do like that, darling. I can feel it all the way down."

"Down where?" he responded.

"Down you know where."

"No, I don't." He grinned. "Tell me."

"I can feel it all the way down into my pussy. Is that what you want to hear, Custis?"

"What I always want t' hear, darlin', is the truth, always the truth." He slid toward the foot of the bed and began to lick and suck at her nipples, kneading the pliant flesh with his hand while he did so.

His hand left her breast and slid down across her belly. Into the soft mat of her bush. And beyond, into her pussy.

Liz gasped and arched her back to make his entry easier.

He toyed with her clitoris and quickly the lady cried out aloud as she reached a sudden climax.

"That's not fair," she said. "Now you've gone and taken the edge off."

"Oh, I think I know how t' put it back," he said, smiling.

"Can you prove that?" she challenged.

"Damn right I can."

Liz reached for Longarm's cock. She wrapped her fingers around it and squeezed, then reached down lower and began to tickle his balls with her fingernails.

"Does that feel good?" she asked.

"You know it does, darlin'," he said.

"Would you like me to suck this beautiful thing?" Liz asked.

"Is that an offer, honey, or jus' curiosity?"

"Oh, it's an offer, all right. I want to taste your come. I want to drink it," she said.

By way of an answer Longarm laid his hand on the back of Liz's head and gently pushed her down toward his cock, which by now was rock hard and pulsing lightly with each heartbeat.

Elizabeth practically purred with pleased eagerness as she licked her way down across his belly to his cock. She ran the tip of her tongue up and down his shaft, then probed inside his foreskin. She took him into her mouth, the heat of her engulfing and tantalizing him.

Then she began pushing herself onto him. She took the head in. Then deeper. And deeper still until he was penetrating past her mouth and into her throat.

Longarm felt his sap rise. He did not try to hold back. Elizabeth continued to suck even as his juices shot into her throat. She sucked it down greedily, making little snuffling, slobbering noises as his come flowed.

And that, he thought, was just the beginning of what promised to be a perfectly lovely evening.

Chapter 38

Longarm woke up, groggy and fuzzy headed. He had no idea what the time was or, for that matter, where he was. Gradually the fog cleared and he realized that he was in his own bed in Hettie's whorehouse.

He had left Elizabeth about two in the morning. It was still dark beyond the small window in his room. Hettie's girls must still be working, he assumed, because some inconsiderate son of a bitch kept pounding on his door.

That, he belatedly realized, was what woke him.

Longarm yawned and rubbed his face and eyes. The inside of his mouth tasted foul and his eyes were gritty, glued nearly shut with sleep.

"Go 'way," he grumbled aloud.

"Marshal. Marshal Long," a voice at the door persisted. "Wake up."

Longarm sat up and blinked a few times trying to clear the cobwebs in his skull.

"Marshal! Come quick!"

That did it. He jumped out of bed and grabbed his britches and his gun belt.

He threw the door open to find a worried-looking man

in sleeve garters and an apron. "He's killing them, Marshal. It's awful. You got to stop it."

"Where's this?" Longarm snapped.

"At the saloon. You got to come, Marshal. We can't control him."

Longarm thundered down the stairs. Hettie's whores, most of them anyway, stood in the parlor doorway staring out at the excitement.

When he reached the street outside Hettie's he automatically turned toward Jacob Potts's saloon. Behind him the bartender who had delivered the frantic request screamed, "No, Marshal, it's across the way in Stonecipher. It's in Jason's place."

He changed direction and charged across the wide street toward the glaring lamplight showing at Jason Potts's establishment. Once there he slowed and took a moment to catch his breath and steady the rhythm of his breathing.

He did not know if he would need a gun to handle this, but one thing he knew for certain sure: A man needs a steady hand on those rare occasions when it takes gunplay to resolve a situation, and a man whose chest is heaving for air is in no shape to reach for his gun.

Longarm took a deep breath. And pushed through the batwings.

Chapter 39

There were things he would rather have seen.

A dozen or so saloon patrons, cowboys most of them, were crowded against the wall to Longarm's right. The long mahogany bar was on his left. Leaning against the bar was a man in overalls, a flannel shirt and a cloth cap. He had a rather wicked-looking skinning knife in his right hand and a small, nickel-plated pistol in his left. He appeared to be a farmer, not a cowboy.

The man with the knife had obviously been busy. One of his victims lay on the floor, curled into a fetal position, trying to hold his guts in. The gray and red coils of intestine had spilled out through a deep cut in his belly, and his blood was soaking into the sawdust that covered the floor planks.

Past him, past the man with the knife, two others cowered against the front of the bar. It appeared that they wanted to get past the knife-wielding man but were being prevented from doing so.

The bartender, a man named Revis, although Longarm did not know if that was his first name or last, was behind his bar, standing well clear of the loco farmer with the knife.

Of the two cowboys who were being held at bay by the man in overalls, at least one of them had been cut. He was holding a bandanna wrapped tight around his wrist. Blood dripped off his fingertips into the sawdust.

Longarm could not see if his companion had been cut, but from the way that fellow stood hunched over with his arms wrapped tight around his stomach considered it a very strong likelihood.

"You!" Longarm barked. "Drop the knife an' the gun. Do it pronto."

The man in the overalls looked at him and blinked a little. He did not drop either weapon.

"Did you cut these men?"

Again there was no answer, just a vacant stare.

"He did, Marshal," the bartender said. "I think he's killed young Ben there." The man pointed toward the fellow lying curled up on the floor. "And he's cut these two, too."

"I got to get to a doctor, mister, but the big son of a bitch won't let me past," the second of the two cowboys at the bar said.

"He cut me too, Marshal, but not so bad as Leon here. He's crazy, loony as a horned toad," the nearer said. He was the one standing closer to the belligerent fellow so it took some balls to risk insulting him.

Neither of the cowboys was wearing a pistol or Longarm suspected the confrontation would not have gone on this long, and of the few others in the room who were armed no one seemed inclined to step in and do something about the situation. But then it was the marshal's job to risk himself and they all knew it.

"Put the knife an' the gun on the bar," Longarm told the farmer. "An' apologize for what you done here tonight."

"These bastards was making fun of me," the farmer mumbled.

"What? I couldn't hear you," Longarm said.

He repeated the comment and added, "They deserve to die for making fun of a man."

"Maybe they do deserve it," Longarm said. "I wouldn't

know 'bout that. But I do know it ain't your place t' decide it. I ain't, either. That's for a proper judge an' jury. So do like I said. Put the knife an' the gun on the bar an' come with me."

"Where?" the farmer demanded.

"Over to the jail," Longarm told him. He smiled. "You got the honor o' being the very first man ever put behind those bars."

"Is that an honor? Really?"

Longarm could not decide if the man was being facetious or not. Not that it made any difference. "Yeah, 'tis," he said.

The fellow seemed to turn that over in his mind for a few seconds. Then he grinned. Turned. Laid both his knife and his pistol on the bar. "All right," he said. "I'll go with you. I heard about that jail of yours. Now I'll get to see it."

"Let's do this proper," Longarm said. "Turn around an' put your hands behind you so's I can put the handcuffs on you."

The farmer obediently turned and stuck both hands behind his back. At which point Longarm realized he did not have any handcuffs with him after jumping up out of bed and rushing across the street.

"For now," he said, "we'll have t' pretend you're wearing cuffs. Would that be all right?"

"Why?"

Longarm explained.

"Oh. Then . . . sure, that will be all right." And he marched outside and off toward the jail with his hands held awkwardly behind his back.

Longarm shrugged. And followed.

Someone else would have to take care of the men who had been cut. Longarm wanted to get the farmer behind bars, then he could come back and see if the fellow would be charged with assault. Or with murder.

Chapter 40

Longarm got the door open but there was no light burning inside. With no prisoners in the jail there had not been any reason to burn oil overnight. He turned to his prisoner and said, "Wait here while I find a match. I forgot t' grab mine when they rousted me out o' sleep."

"I have some," the man offered.

"Thanks." Longarm accepted a pair of matches from the farmer and went inside, the prisoner close behind.

He felt his way to the desk and struck a match, pulled the lamp close, and touched the flame to the wick. A warm yellow light filled the small room.

"Back there." Longarm motioned toward the cell at the back of the jail.

The prisoner walked inside docilely enough but when Longarm moved to close the cell door the man's eyes became wide and he shook his head vehemently from side to side. "No, sir," he bawled.

"What?"

"Don't . . . don't close me in like that. I can't stand to be closed in."

"Mister, you can see right past these bars. You shouldn't have a closed-in feeling about this."

"No. Really. No."

"I got to . . ."

Longarm did not have time to finish his sentence about what he had to do. The farmer stood up and bellowed, a roar that was not formed into words. And needed none.

Before Longarm could get the door latched shut the prisoner lunged, hands grasping, lips drawn back in a snarl.

And with a knife in his hand. Another knife that he had been carrying under the bib of his overalls.

Longarm had not thought to search the seemingly cooperative fellow. Now it was too late. Much too late.

Longarm swung the cell door shut in his face, but the man crashed through it, pushed it back into Longarm, who stumbled backward and nearly fell.

The prisoner lashed out with his knife blade, swinging and slashing crazily. It must have been the way he attacked those men in the saloon. Longarm did not want to wind up the same way—lying on the saloon floor. Not only did he not want to, he had no intention of it.

He sidestepped another swing of the knife blade and went for his Colt.

The sound of the big .45's muzzle blast filled the small jail building and momentarily destroyed Longarm's hearing.

A lead slug driven by forty grains of black powder struck the farmer in the brisket and knocked him to his knees.

The man looked up at Longarm. His mouth formed a wide O but no sound came out.

He looked down at the knife he still held in his right hand. Then he toppled forward on top of the weapon.

His feet drummed on the floorboards briefly and then he was gone.

"Shit," Longarm muttered. He knelt beside the dead man and turned him over to retrieve the knife, which he put away on one of the little shelves built on the side of his desk in lieu of drawers.

He had not even gotten the man's name.

Longarm drew the dead man's legs out straight and crossed his arms over his belly, then pressed the eyes closed.

Finally he stood and went out into the pale starlight. He needed to go see to the situation at the saloon, see if the gutted man was dead and how badly the other two were hurt.

All that and he still had no idea what started the altercation. But then it was a saloon fight and the cause scarcely mattered anyway.

Longarm felt weary and a hundred years old as he walked slowly back toward Jason Potts's saloon.

Chapter 41

"You had some trouble last night," Jacob Potts said, sliding onto a stool at Longarm's side.

Longarm nodded. "At your brother's place."

"Yeah, that's what I heard," Potts said, "although I thought at first it was just a rumor. So there's a prisoner in our jail this morning?"

Longarm picked up an undersized pitcher of fresh milk and poured some into his coffee, then dumped the rest over his bowl of porridge, adding a generous measure of sugar on top of that.

"No prisoner," he said. "Which reminds me. I need t' clean the floor in there, get rid o' all that blood if I can."

"What happened?" Potts asked.

"I'm s'prised you ain't heard. You seem to get all the news from the other side of the line easy enough. Come t' think of it, how *do* you hear what goes on over there if there ain't no back and forth between you?"

Potts looked away. "A man just sort of hears things. Especially a man in my position. You know?"

"But how'd you hear this particular thing this mornin'?" Longarm persisted.

"Why, I think, um, I believe George might have

mentioned it." He paused for a moment, then nodded as if to himself. "Yes, I'm pretty sure it was George who said something about it."

"And he would know about it how?" Longarm asked.

"I don't really know, but our customers, Jason's and mine, do sometimes cross the street."

"I thought the cowboys were pretty much confined to one side or t'other," Longarm said.

"They are, for the most part, but there is no law about it. And sometimes a man will want to come over to this side, like if he wants to change what brand he rides for or if he is just riding the grub line looking for work." Potts smiled. "Not everyone around here works for one side or the other. Strangers passing through wouldn't know or care about our ways, Marshal. They could carry tales back and forth."

"Or that old fellow selling water. He sells on both sides of the line, doesn't he?" Longarm said.

"Wallace Waterman, you mean," Potts said. "Yes, he sells to both sides. We tolerate him." Potts scratched the beard stubble beneath his chin. "Come to think of it, we could forbid Wallace to sell on the other side. The thirst might drive them away and then we would be left alone to do as we please."

"How are the Nebraska people displeasing you as it is?" Longarm asked.

"Why, um, well," Potts blinked rapidly, "they just sort of . . . do."

"'Scuse me, Jacob. My porridge is getting cold."

"Yes, of course." Potts stood, hesitated for a moment, then walked out of the café. Longarm returned to his rapidly cooling breakfast.

Chapter 42

Longarm spent the day being seen on both sides of the line, had supper on the Nebraska side, then paid Liz a visit.

"I was hoping you would come for supper," she told him when he got there. "I had a place at the table laid for you."

He smiled and took the lady into his arms. "Then how's about we settle for dessert instead."

Liz's tongue fluttered inside his mouth as she reached for the buttons at his fly. And for what lay behind those buttons.

An hour later Longarm sat up and reached for a cheroot.

"Sleep here tonight," Liz said. "I love sleeping next to you. I love the smell of you, the warmth. Please stay."

He flicked a match aflame and used it to get the slender cigar lighted, then exhaled a cloud of aromatic smoke. "I better not," he said. "If I happen t' be needed, like I was last night, it's best if they don't find me sleepin' in your bed. Besides, I got my rounds to make. Got to make sure all the proper doors are locked and there ain't no burglars about."

"If you change your mind . . ."

"I'll know where t' come," he said, leaning down to give the girl a kiss.

Longarm took his time with the cigar, then dressed and gave Liz one last kiss. Which threatened to last until morning, but he reluctantly pulled himself away and said, "I got to go now. Really, darlin'."

He let himself out, knowing his way in the dark by now, and made sure the latch caught behind him. He paused for a moment on the porch, enjoying the cool of the night, then made his way across toward the jail.

The bright yellow of a muzzle flash blossomed in the night from beside the jail, and a bullet sizzled past his left ear like the buzz of the world's largest—and nastiest—bee ever.

Longarm hit the ground, Colt ready in his hand.

He heard the distant, muted thud of running footsteps.

Then the night air was silent but not so comfortably so as it had been just a few minutes earlier.

Some son of a bitch was gunning for him, seriously gunning this time, but he had no idea who. Nor why. He had placed only two men under arrest since he came to town and both of them were dead now.

But someone wanted him out of the way. He had no doubts about that. Someone wanted Deputy U.S. Marshal Custis Long dead.

Chapter 43

He rose to his feet and made his way across the ruts of the central street. Checked the door of the jail. It was not locked, but then there had been no need to lock it earlier and he had left it that way.

A quick check inside found nothing out of place, at least nothing that was obvious.

There certainly was no one lurking inside with a gun in hand. He rather wished there had been. It would have been a pleasure for him to shoot the son of a bitch.

Lacking that, he walked back to the Nebraska side of the street and checked the doors along the sidewalk and around back through the alley. From there he crossed over to Wyoming and did the same on that side of the street.

The only businesses that were open were the Potts brothers' saloons, and those would stay open as long as there were customers. There was no law on either side to specify when a saloon could be open for business, so they were apt to stay all night if there was someone wanting to drink.

Longarm wondered if the unknown gunman had fled from beside the jail to refuge in Jacob's saloon. He very likely had, but customers were coming and going on a fairly regular basis at this hour so it would not be possible to identify the bastard that way.

Still, he gave it a try. George Griner could not remember the comings and goings of his customers.

"To tell you the truth, Marshal, unless I happen to know a man I don't pay any attention to their faces. They order a drink; I serve it, but I don't pay much attention to who's drinking what."

Longarm grunted. He supposed that was possible. Although a genuinely good bartender not only knew the customers, he remembered what they drank. Longarm had known a man tending bar in Las Cruces, New Mexico, who served him a brandy flip one winter day. A year and a half later Longarm happened to walk into the same bar. The bartender immediately asked if he wanted another flip. Now *that*, Longarm thought, was a bartender.

George Griner was not in that man's league and likely never would be.

But he was what Valmere and Jacob Potts had so he would just have to do.

Just to be sure, Longarm walked across to Jason's place and asked the barman there the same question. He got the same answer from Revis as he had from Griner.

"I'm sorry, Marshal, but we've been busy this evening. There's been a steady flow. Fellas coming and going. I can't keep track of them. D'you want a beer or a whiskey or something?"

"I could stand a beer," Longarm said. At least here on the Nebraska side he could get a good one, unlike across the street in Wyoming.

Revis drew one for him and Longarm took his time with it, standing with both elbows on the bar and facing into the room. He watched the crowd as they did indeed amble in and out, no one paying any particular mind to his presence.

Eventually Longarm gave up and headed for his bed across the way in Stella's.

At least this time no one shot at him.

Chapter 44

It was pitch-black in his room when he wakened to a sensation of wet heat in his groin. His dick was hard so he must have been dreaming.

Then he heard a series of soft, slurping sounds to go with the sense of urgency in his cock.

Longarm smiled. And let himself relax to the sensations of a very deep, warm, wet, and experienced blow job.

He had no idea who had slipped into his room and started sucking him, but whoever it was was very good. Quiet, too, to be able to come into his room like that.

Longarm lay back and enjoyed what the girl was doing. Her touch was delicate, so soft he did not think she could bring him off. Especially after he was with Liz earlier in the evening. She had taken the edge off of his needs. Off his needs but not his desires.

He arched his back and pushed deeper into the girl's warm, wet mouth. Into the mouth and through to her throat, which he could feel tight around the head of his cock.

With a groan and a lurch of his hips, Longarm shot his cum, spewing hot into her throat.

The girl made a faint gobbling sound and grabbed at him

so that for a moment he thought he must have hurt her, but she swallowed before she pulled away.

His cock felt cold when the night air found the moisture she had left behind. It sank back to its normal size, and he felt the girl kiss his dick and his belly.

"Thank you," he said softly. "That was nice."

"Good," she said. "I wanted it to be."

Longarm rolled onto one elbow and ran his hand over the back of her head.

"Do you mind if I light the lamp?" he asked. "I'd like t' see who you are."

"No, it's all right."

He felt on the bedside stand for his matches, struck one, and touched it to the wick of his lamp.

He smiled and caressed the side of the girl's face.

He could not remember this one's name but he had been seeing her daily—nightly, really—ever since he moved into Stella's. She was not pretty, a plump little thing with a bad complexion and small tits, but now he understood why she was so popular with the customers. The girl gave a blow job that was simply outstanding.

"I'd like t' ask you something," he said.

"All right."

"Why?"

The girl giggled and reached up to pet his flaccid cock. "You been here all this time, living right amongst us, but you never made a pass at any of us. We was beginning to think there was something wrong with you. Like maybe you got your dick shot off in a gunfight or something. So we was talking about this and decided one of us should come find out. We drew straws and I came up the winner." She laughed and added, "Now I can go back and tell all the girls that there's not a thing in the world wrong with your dick. No, ma'am, there isn't." She touched it again, lightly stroking it.

"Careful," he said. "Keep that up an' you'll wake the wolf."

"Promise?" she said.

"Promise."

With a bubbly grin she began to suck him again. Once Longarm was erect she pulled away and said, "This time I'd like to feel it in my pussy if you don't mind." With a sigh she said, "It's such a pretty thing."

"I don't mind," he assured her. "Now come up here beside me on this here bed."

The girl threw her chemise aside and, naked, came to him.

Chapter 45

Longarm whipped up a nice froth in his soap mug and used his brush to plaster it onto his face. He lighted a cheroot to fill the time while he waited for the shaving soap to soften his beard stubble.

His thoughts inevitably went to the girl who had come into his room during the night. It had not occurred to him until she was gone that he never got around to asking her name. Not that he supposed that mattered. She gave a great blow job and was a wildcat in bed. What more would a boy need to know?

He set the cigar aside, ran his razor several times back and forth across a strop, and commenced to carefully shave. When he was done with that he used a hand towel—whorehouses are well equipped with towels if with nothing else—to wipe the remaining soap from his face.

Taking a pair of small, sharp scissors from his bag, he trimmed his mustache, then dampened a corner of the towel, dipped that into a tin of salt and scrubbed his teeth. A quick run of a brush over his hair and he was ready to face a new day.

It would be nice, he thought, if he could get through it without being shot at.

No, he corrected himself, it would be nice if he could catch the son of a bitch who was shooting at him. So far he had no idea who that might be. Or why.

He pulled his shirt over his head—he really had to remember to send his laundry down today—tucked it into his trousers and slipped his suspenders over his shoulders.

Longarm buckled his gun belt around his hips and from long habit eased the heavy Colt out a few inches to make sure it was free in the leather, then carefully seated it again, ready for instant use if that should be required.

He quickly fastened his collar and tie, picked up his hat and put it on, then finally reached for his coat and shrugged into it.

Who, damnit? Why? The questions kept hounding him, but there was nothing he could do to satisfy them. Not at the moment, he couldn't.

Longarm went downstairs and outside, then turned toward the Valmere side of town, heading to the café and some breakfast, ready to start a new day.

Chapter 46

"Marshal, there's a fight brewing over at the mercantile," the nearly breathless boy shouted.

Longarm stood. "Which side o' town, son?" There were two general stores, one on each side of the line, just like pretty much everything else around here, and he had learned by now to make sure he was dashing off to the correct side of town before he did the dashing.

"Wyoming, sir."

He grabbed his Stetson off the peg he had put into the wall beside the doorway and headed at a lope for Garrett Franz's store.

When he got there he found Franz facing off with a red-faced and obviously very angry cowboy. The cowboy was a good head taller than Franz, and his posture was threatening. Like most cowhands he carried a pistol on his hip when he was in town, although he might not have bothered with the weight and the nuisance when he was working. Franz was not armed, which likely saved him from the young cowboy's fury.

"You're a cheating son of a bitch," the cowboy bawled, his voice cracking.

"Call me whatever you like," Franz snapped back at him,

"but you asked me to perform a service and I did so. It's too late now for you to balk at the price."

"You deliberately cheated me, damn you," the cowboy shouted.

For a moment Longarm thought the young man was going for his gun. Longarm's .45 was in his hand and ready to bark, but all the cowboy did was scratch his belly. He never actually touched the butt of his Colt.

Garrett Franz must have had the same impression as Longarm. Presumably assuming that his customer was reaching for his gun, Franz lashed out at the tall young man, burying his fist in the cowboy's belly.

Longarm expected the cowboy to respond by beating the crap out of the shopkeeper. Certainly that was what most rugged young men would have done. Instead the boy doubled over, holding his stomach with both hands and dropping to his knees.

That behavior seemed odd. Until Longarm saw the young fellow's blood spilling out onto the rough planks of the floor.

And saw the now-bloody blade of a knife in Garret Franz's fist. The shopkeeper had been hiding a stinger beneath his apron.

"You saw him, Marshal," Franz said calmly. "He was going for his gun. I only defended myself. You saw. You were standing right there. You saw it all."

The cowboy continued to clutch his stomach. He looked up, tears streaming down his cheeks, but he said nothing.

"Put that thing away, Franz, an' help me get him over to the jail," Longarm said, nodding in the direction of the knife that Franz continued to hold.

"What? Oh, uh, yes, of course." Franz tucked the blade away somewhere under his apron, grabbed the cowboy by the arms and yanked the young fellow to his feet.

"Where do you want him, Marshal?"

"We'll take him over to the jail. I can stretch him out on one o' the bunks."

Longarm got on one side of the cowboy and Franz took the other. Between them they half carried, half walked the cowboy out of the general store and down the street to the jail.

"In there," Longarm said, pointing to the lone cell at the back of the little building. They took the cowboy into the cell and laid him on the crude bunk.

When they stepped back out, leaving the cowboy there, Franz said, "For what it is worth, Marshal, Bobby there is banned from my shop. Permanently."

"What was he arguing about?" Longarm asked.

"He wanted a pair a chaps made with his personal brand inlayed on the right leg and his initials on the left. I had to take the chaps out of my stock and send them down to Cheyenne to have the work done. I don't do it myself, you understand. I had the chaps made up to his exact specifications and paid the shoemaker . . . the fellow who did the actual work . . . out of my own pocket. Bobby became upset when I told him the price. You saw the result."

"Yes," Longarm said. "So I did." He also thought, but did not say out loud, that he was anxious to hear the cowboy, Bobby something, give his side of the story.

Longarm saw Franz out, then returned to the cell where Bobby something lay curled up into a tight ball on the rough planks of the bunk.

Chapter 47

"Sir?" The voice was weak but at least the young fellow was awake now. Longarm got up and went into the cell. He sat on the edge of the bunk where Bobby lay.

"Yeah, kid?"

"You . . . you're the marshal?"

Longarm nodded. "I am."

"You'll tell me straight, won't you? Am I gonna die?"

Longarm smiled down at the worried youngster. "Hell, kid, we're all of us gonna die. Eventually."

"I . . . I mean . . ."

"Oh, I know what you mean an' if I could tell you I would. But I just don't know. It all depends on what got punctured in there. I've seen a man shot in the gut with a .50-caliber Sharps an' live. On the other hand I've seen a man keel over an' die without no reason at all, 'least none that I could figure. How do you feel?"

Bobby reflected on the question for a moment before he answered. "Like I got a bellyache," he said finally.

"How bad?"

"Pretty bad, sir. Can I have something to drink, sir?"

"I seem t' recall bein' told once that a man with a belly

wound shouldn't have nothing to drink. An' you don't have to call me 'sir,' " Longarm said.

"Whoever told you that didn't have a hole in his gut," Bobby said.

"You have a point. I wouldn't think a little whiskey would hurt. Might help damp the pain down some." He smiled. "I just happen t' have a bottle I brought over from the saloon."

"Which side, sir?"

Longarm laughed. "You aren't so bad off, I'm thinking, if you can think about that. An' it came from the Nebraska side."

"In that case, sir, I'd sure like to have me a drink."

Longarm stood up and went out into the office side of the room to fetch the bottle he had purchased from Jason Potts. He got it and returned to the cell. "Can you sit up?" he asked.

"Yes, sir." Bobby levered himself upright, still holding his belly with one hand.

Longarm pulled the cork and handed him the bottle. "I don't have a glass for you."

Bobby smiled. "That's all right, sir."

"Tell me something, kid. If all you cowboys know about the difference in the quality o' the liquor on the two sides o' the street, how's come you always stay to the one side or the other an' don't never cross over to get the best deal or the best liquor?"

Bobby took a healthy pull on the bottle, then shrugged. "I don't really know, sir. That's just the way it is. Our outfit always sticks to the Wyoming side. Always have." He took another drink.

"Is that helping you any?" Longarm asked.

"Yes, sir. Some. It's easing the pain a mite." He drank again, deeper this time, then returned the bottle to Longarm. "Here, sir. I shouldn't be drinking up all your whiskey."

"Keep it if you like. I know where I can get more." Longarm smiled. "From the Nebraska side."

Bobby grinned. And took another swallow.

"Listen, I have a deck o' cards an' a board if you want to play cribbage or something," Longarm offered.

The infectious grin returned. "I'll beat you, sir. I'm pretty good at cribbage. We play it in the bunkhouse a lot."

"That ain't gonna happen." Longarm laughed. "'Specially if I get you good an' drunk. Have another taste o' that bottle there."

"I will. And you, sir, get your board so I can whup you at cribbage, drunk or not."

Longarm went to get the makings of a game.

Chapter 48

Come evening Longarm had Harrison McPhail at the Nebraska side café boil a bowl of porridge for Bobby and carried it to him on a tray loaded with sugar and canned milk.

Bobby cocked his head to one side and closed one eye as he peered at his supper. "To tell you the truth, sir, I was hoping for something a little more substantial. A steak, maybe, and fried taters."

"Let's see how that belly of yours does. I don't want t' push your luck," Longarm told the young cowboy. "How's it feel now?"

"Pretty bad, sir."

Longarm had tried throughout the day to get Bobby to quit calling him "sir," but it had been to no avail. The boy persisted with it. "Is it hurting any less than it was this morning, kid?"

He shook his head. "Worse, if anything."

"We better hold off on the steak and spuds then." Longarm smiled. During their afternoon together he had come to like the boy. "Tell you what. If you're feeling any better come morning, I'll have Harry fix you that steak and the fried taters, too. Maybe some of his dried apple pie t' go with it."

"That sounds fine, sir."

"But for now the porridge will have t' do. All right?"

"Yes, sir." Bobby laced his oatmeal heavy with milk and sugar, then picked up the spoon and dug in.

Later Longarm asked him if he wanted to play some more cribbage.

"Thank you, sir, but if it's all the same to you I'll lie down here and kind of get my strength back. And, Marshal, there's something I want you to know. This afternoon over at Mr. Franz's store . . . I wasn't going for my gun, sir. I was mad, but I'm no killer. I wouldn't do a thing like that."

"Hell, I already knew that, kid."

"Yes, sir, I figured. But I wanted to say it anyhow. Just to like . . . get it on the record, sort of."

"Do you need anything more, Bobby?" Earlier Longarm had walked over to the whorehouse and borrowed a pillow and two blankets for the boy to use. He certainly was not going anywhere for a while and would need them.

"No, sir, I'm fine."

"All right then. I'm going to leave the door unlocked and this lamp burning. I filled it fresh with oil this afternoon so it should last you through the night. I'll put the bucket beside you in case you have t' go during the night. Don't try an' make it to the outhouse without me bein' here to help. Is there anything else you can think of before I leave?"

"No, sir, thank you."

"I still have a job t' do here so I need to make my rounds an' stop in at both saloons to make sure everybody remembers to mind their manners. An' I'm hungry, too, so I'd best take care o' that while I'm out. I, uh, I might not have a chance t' get back here for a while. Are you sure you're all right?"

"I'm fine, sir."

"All right then, Bobby. Good night."

"Good night, sir."

Longarm left the cell door standing open and set the latch on the outside door but did not lock it. That done, he tugged the brim of his hat down and headed back to McPhail's Café to take care of his own supper.

In the morning, Longarm found Bobby curled on the bunk where he had left him.

The boy was dead, his flesh cold enough to indicate he had been gone for some hours.

"Damnit!" Longarm cried out aloud. "Damn it all to hell an' gone."

Chapter 49

"Serves the little bastard right," Garrett Franz said with a snort when Longarm told him about Bobby's death.

"It doesn't bother you that you killed a man yesterday?" Longarm said, incredulous.

"Of course not. He went for his six-shooter. You were standing right there, Marshal. You saw."

"Yes, I did see," Longarm said, "and what I saw wasn't Bobby reaching for a gun. What I saw was you committing murder with that knife o' yours."

Franz puffed up like a toad in heat, stuck out both his chest and his chin, and declared, "You go to thinking like that, Marshal, and you'll find yourself out of a job. This town can fire you as easy as hire you."

Longarm snorted. "Garrett, you've forgot somethin' here. This town never hired me t' begin with. I work for U.S. Marshal William Vail, not you. If Billy wants t' fire me, that's one thing. If you want to, well, lots o' luck with that. You got nothing t' say about the job I do here. Now I'm gonna give you a job. You killed that boy so you take care o' collecting his body from out of the jail an' seeing to his burying. An' while you're at it, see that his outfit is told that he's dead. What bunch did he ride for anyhow?"

"Bobby was a XOX," Franz said.

"An' while I think about it, see that the boy is laid out and buried wearing those chaps he wanted."

"Those chaps cost me—"

Longarm's voice was as hard as ice when he interrupted. "I don't give a fat shit what they cost, Franz, they're of no use to you nor anybody else, made up with Bobby's brand an' initials. So do it."

"You can't tell me . . .".

"I just did. Now *do it*!"

The storekeeper did not look happy although Longarm could not tell whether the man was more aggravated by the loss of the custom-made chaps or by being told what to do by someone he obviously thought of as a town employee.

Not that it mattered and not that Custis Long gave that fat shit he had mentioned. Despite what Garrett Franz seemed to think, Longarm was not there to please the community leaders but to do the job of keeping the peace and enforcing such laws as there were.

"I assume the laying out will be here in the store. Dress him in those chaps an' lay him out this afternoon. Send someone to tell the XOX so's they can attend the buryin' if they're of a mind to. Don't do that until his compadres have had a chance t' see him."

Franz looked completely taken aback to be given orders like that, but he said nothing more.

When Longarm left the mercantile he left Garrett Franz fuming behind him.

Chapter 50

Longarm did not know if Franz complied with his instruction to notify Bobby's bunkmates or if someone else spread the word, but that afternoon the XOX riders, eight of them, came boiling into town with trouble on their minds.

When they arrived Longarm was on the Nebraska side making a show of being on duty. As soon as he saw the XOXs he hustled across to Wyoming. When he got there Garrett Franz was rather nervously explaining himself to the obviously unhappy XOX cowhands.

"There," Franz said, pointing toward Longarm, who was just coming in the doorway. "There's the marshal. He saw it all. Your friend Bobby was going for his gun. Ask the marshal."

"Well?" demanded one of the XOX crew, a short, sun-baked man with a Smith & Wesson break top worn cross-draw style.

"Who are you t' be asking?" Longarm returned.

"I'm Timothy Wilcox. I'm foreman of the XOX."

Longarm nodded and introduced himself.

"Marshal, we know . . . that is, we knew . . . Bobby Reims. He wasn't the sort to gun a man down no matter the provocation. He was a good kid. We knew him though maybe you didn't," Wilcox said.

"I got t' know him some while he was with me. I liked him," Longarm said, "an' I was sad to see him pass."

"What about what this man says?" Wilcox said. "What about him saying Bobby tried to draw on him?"

"Mr. Wilcox, I can't never tell you what another man was thinkin'. If Franz says he thought Bobby was drawing, well, maybe he did think that," Longarm said.

"What about you, Marshal? What did you think?"

"Me, I didn't think so. But then I wasn't the one standing in front o' him there. If Franz was scared, that's up to him."

"String him up," one of the cowboys shouted.

That brought a chorus of loud calls for Garrett Franz to be hanged.

The storekeeper shrank back against some shelving on his back wall and reached under his apron.

"There will be no lynchings here," Longarm said, his voice and his demeanor steely. "No one is gonna touch that man."

The XOX hands all looked to Wilcox for guidance. Longarm was sure if Tim Wilcox gave the nod, his riders would do their best to tear Franz limb from limb and then hang whatever was left.

Wilcox, for his part, looked to Longarm. "Arrest him, Marshal. What he done was murder plain and simple."

"I can't do it," Longarm said. "I think he was wrong, but I can't say that was intentional. He ain't done nothing for me t' arrest him for. What I suggest you boys do is t' take your man an' bury him." Looking squarely at Garrett Franz he added, "An' make sure he's wearing those fancy chaps he wanted so bad. The boy is entitled t' that much consideration."

"I'll go get them," Franz said quickly.

"Where is Bobby?" Wilcox asked.

"He's laying over in the jail. It's open."

"We didn't come here to cause any trouble," the XOX foreman said. "We just want our man. But I can tell you one thing. From now on the XOX will be doing its business across the way. Maybe we'll be treated better over on that side."

"Every penny," one of the cowboys put in.

"What about the whorehouses?" someone else asked. "Do we have to cross over for that, too?"

"I got me a special gal at Stella's," another said.

Wilcox drew himself up to his full height and said, "Everything. From now on we give our trade in Nebraska." He nodded toward Franz. "This slimy son of a bitch is partners in Stella's place. He won't be getting none of our pay, not from now on."

"Come along," Longarm said. "I'll walk with you over to the jail. You." He pointed to one of the XOX hands. "You get those chaps from Franz here an' bring them over to the jail so's we can rig Bobby out proper."

"Yes, sir, Marshal." The young cowboy turned and got in Garrett Franz's face like he was hoping the storekeeper would refuse and give him an excuse to cause some mayhem, but Franz meekly ducked under his counter and came up with the paper wrapped bundle that had been the cause of all the trouble.

"Come with me, fellas," Longarm encouraged as he led the XOX riders out of the store and up the street toward the jail. Which still had not had a prisoner inside its bars.

Chapter 51

"You cleaned him up real nice, Marshal. We XOXs appreciate that," Wilcox said. "Thank you."

"I liked the boy," Longarm told them.

Three of the XOX cowboys stepped forward to wrestle Bobby into his chaps and tidy up his clothing. There was practically no blood for them to deal with. Virtually all of the bleeding from Franz's knife had been contained inside the body, which was why Longarm had not realized the wound was a mortal one.

The only visible indication on the corpse was a small cut just below and to the right of his navel.

"He was a likeable kid," Wilcox commented as Bobby's bunkmates were busy strapping his fancy chaps in place.

"He was that," Longarm agreed.

"You sure there's no cause to arrest that bastard Franz?"

"I'm sure," Longarm said. He raised his voice a little. "Something else I'm sure of. The man who tries t' get revenge on behalf o' Bobby will either hang or go down in front o' my guns. I'll make sure o' that my own self."

"Point taken," Wilcox said. He turned to his crew. "Little Bit, bring the wagon around. We'll take him home to bury him." Glancing in the general direction of Franz's store he said, "I wouldn't want a good man like Bobby Reims lying in dirt anywhere near this place. Better he lays in the sod where he's appreciated."

One of the cowboys, a large man with a mustache that hung down on his chest, touched the brim of his hat to acknowledge the order, then turned and hurried away.

"It will take him a spell to go fetch the wagon. Can we buy you a drink for being so thoughtful to our man, Marshal?" Wilcox offered.

"I'd be honored," Longarm said. "In Nebraska?"

"Aye, though it will gravel us to go over there where we haven't been welcome."

"I think," Longarm said, "you'll find yourselves more welcome there than you might've been led t' believe. Come along then. An' let me buy the second round. That'd be an honor, too."

Chapter 52

"Where exactly did you get the notion that Wyoming cow-boys aren't wanted on the Nebraska side o' town?" Longarm asked over the rim of a passable rye whiskey.

"Why, I don't exactly recall. It's just always been that way, long as we been on this range," Wilcox said. To the others in his crew he asked, "Anybody remember how we was told we wasn't welcome over here on the Nebraska side?"

No one did.

"Interesting," Longarm observed, taking another sip of the whiskey. It was not as good as the Maryland distilled rye he got back home in Denver. But this was not bad on the tongue. And that was just the first glass. Almost any whiskey begins to taste better the more a man has of it. Half a dozen shots and even Jacob Potts's horse piss might commence to taste good.

"Little Bit has the wagon parked outside the jail," one of the hands said from his post beside the batwings.

"Then let's go get our boy and take him home," Wilcox said. The foreman quickly downed his whiskey and chugged the beer chaser.

"I haven't had a chance t' buy a round for your boys," Longarm said.

"Next time, Marshal, we'd be proud to drink your whiskey," Wilcox told him as he headed for the doorway.

Longarm carried his drink to the door after the XOX boys left. He propped himself there and watched, hoping there would be no trouble, while the cow crew went into the jail and gently carried their friend and bunkmate out to the springboard farm wagon.

Then they all mounted up and followed the wagon out of town and off toward the northwest.

There was no trouble.

This time. Longarm was not so sure how they would act the next time they came to town wanting to blow off some steam.

Garrett Franz had damn sure better watch his step that day, Longarm thought, or he might find himself laid out in the back of a wagon himself. And with a sight fewer mourners than Bobby Reims had.

Only when the XOX crowd was out of sight did Longarm turn back to the bar and order another drink.

For some reason he was feeling lonely when he did that. He wondered what Elizabeth Kunsler had planned for dinner and whether she would welcome some company at her table.

Chapter 53

Longarm was feeling considerably better when he left Liz some four hours later. Dinner had been good. Liz had been better. She went with him to the door, still naked and a little bit sweaty, and kissed him good-bye.

"You needed me tonight, Custis," she murmured into his mouth when they kissed. "You really needed me. You can't possibly know how happy that makes me."

He was not entirely sure what Liz meant by that, but if whatever it was made her happy, well, that was good. He kissed her and gave her butt a squeeze and headed out into the night.

He was still acting as town marshal, after all, and needed to make his rounds.

Since he happened to be on the Nebraska side he started there. Walked the board sidewalk in front of all the businesses, checking doors and windows, then swung around behind the line of buildings and did the same thing in the back alleyway.

Everything was secure except for the saloon and whorehouse so he crossed over to the Wyoming side and started toward the alley behind those businesses.

Before he reached the first of them the muzzle blast from

a large-caliber rifle flared in the deep shadows behind Jacob
Potts's saloon.

Longarm threw himself flat, .45 in hand before he hit the
ground. He was blinded by the bright flare and could not
see to shoot.

Then it was too late. He heard running footsteps recede
somewhere ahead. Heard an angry shout although whether
that was because the shooter bumped into someone or
because it was the shooter himself unhappy for having
missed his shot, Longarm could not know.

He lay there for several achingly long moments, blinking
and rubbing his eyes, trying to will his night vision back.

It did return but not quickly enough for him to catch even
a glimpse of whoever it was that shot at him.

A burglar interrupted in the middle of breaking into one
of the closed businesses? Or perhaps an assassin who wanted
no law interfering in the affairs of Valmere, Wyoming. It
could have been either of those. Or something else entirely.

Eventually, his night vision restored, Longarm stood and
shoved his .45 back into the leather.

"Shit," he mumbled.

He meant that literally.

When he hit the ground he landed belly down on a pile
of horse turds.

Now he needed to bathe and change clothes. But first he
had to finish making his rounds of the businesses on the
Wyoming side.

After that he could return to his room at Stella's to clean
up and get some sleep.

Grumpy now, he headed deeper into the alley, rattling
doors and checking for open windows as he went.

Chapter 54

"Something's going on here, Otis, but damned if I know what it might be," Longarm grumbled to the blacksmith when he went to get his horse that morning.

There was nowhere in particular that he needed to go, but he just wanted out of the confines of the border town for a little while.

"If you figure it out," Reed said, "let us know. The folks hereabout will be interested."

Longarm swung his saddle onto the gray, dropped the cinch, reached under the horse's belly to retrieve the loose end, and slipped the latigo through the steel ring woven onto the end of the cinch. He pulled it snug and let the near stirrup down before leading the horse out of the barn and onto the central road.

"If anyone is looking for you, when should I say you'll be back?" Reed asked.

Longarm shrugged. "Damn if I know exactly, but I won't be long. Just want t' get some clean air in my lungs. For sure I'll be back by lunchtime." He stepped into the saddle and sorted the reins between his fingers.

The blacksmith nodded and touched his forehead in silent

salute, then stepped back away from the gray. "Enjoy your morning, Marshal."

Longarm touched his heels to the gray's sides, and the horse stepped out and then quickened to a smooth jog.

With no particular destination in mind he found himself once again wandering in the direction of the lake north of town. He passed Wallace Waterman on his way, the water carrier headed south with more barrels of fresh water to feed the needs of both the Wyoming and Nebraska towns.

"Mornin'," Longarm greeted. "Say, d'you mind if I water my horse on your property while you're away?"

"That'd be all right, Marshal, long as he bends down . . ."

"I know. As long as I don't lift it up to him," Longarm said.

Wallace nodded emphatically. "That's the law." While he sat there on the seat of his battered wagon he kept kneading his upper arms. "I know the law, Marshal."

"Indeed it is," Longarm agreed. "I won't lift any water to him, I promise."

"That's all right then." Wallace took up his driving lines again and shook them out to get his rig moving. "Have a pleasant day, Marshal," he said by way of parting.

Wallace continued on south while Longarm rode north along the well-traveled path to the lake that supplied all the water for both towns.

He dismounted and led the gray down to the water's edge. The horse dropped its head and drank deeply of the cool water.

Longarm let the animal have its fill, then led it back up onto the crest of the low hill that lay just to the east of the lake. He lighted a cheroot and sat cross-legged on the grass, gazing out over the sparkling water while songbirds flitted back and forth among the cattails.

The scene was peaceful and serene, just what he needed, he thought. It seemed a shame the whole town could not . . .

Longarm jumped to his feet with an exclamation that was loud enough to startle some nearby birds.

"Son of a bitch!"

He tossed his cheroot down and swung onto the gray's back, wheeling the horse abruptly back around and spurring it into a gallop toward the south, toward the twin towns that were in his charge.

Chapter 55

"Otis, I need a galloper," Longarm said, speaking even before he stepped down from the saddle. "I need a message taken over to Lusk."

"What's up?" the smith said, taking a break from his bellows and wiping sweat off his forehead.

"The last time I was through there I seem t' recall seeing a lumberyard," Longarm said.

Reed nodded. "That's right. Fella named Bob Marlow runs it."

"You know him? Is he on the square?"

"You can trust Bob. And yes, I know him. We both belong to the same fraternal organization. I helped initiate Bob."

"Then maybe you should send the letter asking for the materials I'm wanting." Longarm grinned. "An' there'll be another levy of both manpower and money. Short-term pain, long-term benefit."

"What do you have in mind?" Reed asked, picking up a poker and prodding the coke burning in his forge.

When Longarm told him, the blacksmith laughed out loud.

"Cal, I need a galloper," Longarm said to the Nebraska-side storekeeper. "I need t' get a letter down to Kimball right away."

"I expect we can come up with that," Cal Bonham said.

"Oh, you're gonna have to come up with a hell of a lot more than that. I'll be looking for manpower and money, too. But I need the galloper to start with," Longarm said.

"What do you have in mind?" Bonham asked.

When Longarm told him, the Nebraska storekeeper burst into laughter. "You're serious?"

"Damn right I am," Longarm said. "An' I'll get it done, too. Count on it."

"I think you're out of your mind," Bonham said. "But you can have your galloper. We'll see about the rest."

"Now if you'll excuse me," Longarm said, touching the brim of his Stetson, "I'm gonna go invite myself to lunch."

A short time later, Longarm was saying, "I came over here hopin' to beg a bite to eat." He grinned. "But you look pretty enough to eat your own self. Can I come in?"

"What a silly question, Custis. You are always welcome here. I thought you knew that," Liz said, pushing the screen door open for his entry.

"I might not be after I tell you what I'm up to," Longarm admitted, removing his hat and stepping into the relative cool of Liz's parlor.

"You sound serious," Elizabeth Kunsler said.

"I am. A little nervous, too. I never done anything like this," he said.

"Like what, exactly?"

Longarm grinned. And told her.

Liz chuckled. And said, "You can count on me for a generous contribution to the cause, Custis. Now come along. I haven't had lunch yet so we can talk while we eat. Then afterward . . ." She laughed and patted the bulge at Longarm's crotch.

Chapter 56

"I'm surprised that Wallace Waterman went along with your idea," Otis Reed commented.

"Are you kidding? Once I explained what I had in mind, he jumped at it. He'll make more money this way, with all the merchants in town paying a flat monthly fee, and he won't have to work near so hard doin' it," Longarm said.

They were among a group of Valmere residents who were walking north to the lake, traveling beside three heavy-loaded wagons hauling lumber.

"Does anyone here know how to do this shit?" Garrett Franz grumbled.

"No, but we'll muddle through an' get it done. Just you watch an' see," Longarm said.

"Or watch and not see," Franz snapped.

"Always the optimist, ain't you," Longarm told the Wyoming storekeeper.

"Why are there no workers here from Nebraska?" Franz said.

"You know good an' well they're busy at their end o' things. So would you rather handle a hammer . . . or a pick an' shovel?"

"The way to handle our Garrett," Otis Reed said, "is to tell him to shut up."

Longarm dropped back a little and in a low voice that he hoped only Reed could hear, said, "There's things I'd like t' say to the man. Starting with 'shut up' and going on from there. Going a hell of a long way on from there."

"Garrett can be annoying, but do what the rest of us do, Marshal. Ignore him." Reed chuckled. "Insults run right off him, but ignoring him drives him crazy."

Longarm laughed. "Thanks for the tip."

As they neared the lake, Longarm hurried to catch up with the wagons. He motioned for everyone to gather close around and said, "All right, damnit. Does anybody know how t' build a water tank?" Smiling he added, "Anybody who's here, that is? No? Well, tough shit. We're gonna build it anyhow. An' don't think the Stonecipher folks weren't invited to the dance. They're all busy ditching an' laying pipe."

Three weeks later the towns had the beginnings of a municipal water department. Of course to begin with it consisted only of the elevated water tank and a windmill-driven pump to fill it, but the pipe that would eventually carry fresh, clean water to a centrally located spigot was still a half mile away.

And two days after the tank was completed, before the windmill filled it, someone set fire to it.

Chapter 57

"Marshal Long. Wake up, sir."

Longarm blinked, groaned once or twice, and opened his eyes. One of Hettie's whores was standing over him. She looked upset.

"They want you downstairs, Marshal."

"Thanks, Katie. Let me pull some britches on an' I'll be right down."

He did not take time to wash or clean his teeth, just pulled on some jeans still dirty from helping dig the ditch intended for a water pipe. He also, considering the time and the urgency in Katie's expression, strapped on his revolver.

Once downstairs he discovered a very worried-looking Wallace Waterman—whose name, he had come to find out, was Simon.

"Fire, Marshal. Somebody snuck in and set the water tank afire."

"Is it . . . ?"

"It hasn't burned complete but at least the one support leg was near about destroyed. I managed to put the fire out before the support collapsed, but I wouldn't trust it to hold once we start putting water into the tank."

"I don't s'pose you saw who done it," Longarm said, rubbing his eyes.

Simon shook his head. "Sorry, Marshal, but I didn't."

"You say the fire was out before you left?"

"Yes, sir."

"All right, thanks."

Longarm got his horse out of Otis Reed's corral and hightailed it north to the new water tank that he intended—hoped—would bring harmony and some sense of togetherness to the people of Valmere and of Stonecipher.

It was difficult to see anything by the dim starlight and he had not thought to bring a lantern, but even so he could see that there was extensive damage to the southeasternmost leg of the tower holding the water tank aloft.

Longarm led the horse a little way off and once again squatted on top of the rise there. Watching. Hoping whoever set the fire would return to finish the job.

They did not. Morning found him gritty-eyed and out of sorts.

He rode back down to Valmere and returned the gray to the blacksmith's corral, then went up to his room in Stella's whorehouse to take a shit, wash up, and shave.

Finally he went downstairs and crossed the street to Harrison McPhail's café.

"Hotcakes this morning, Marshal. Can I tempt you?" McPhail greeted.

"Aye, I'd like a double order, Harry."

"I suppose you heard about the fire out at the water tank," the café owner said.

"I did. Went out there this morning, but there wasn't nothing t' see. Nothing that would point to who set it."

"Did they ruin it, Marshal?" one of the other patrons asked from two stools down.

"Not complete," Longarm told him. "They weakened one leg, but we can replace that. I'll get a crew on that today. They'll see that they haven't thrown us off. Soon as the pipe is finished we can hook things together and have water piped right here into town. We'll put a trough out in the center of the street where any man or any horse is welcome. It will work out fine. You'll see."

"I just hope they don't try and burn it again," another customer said.

"I don't reckon they will." Longarm smiled, expressing confidence that he did not at all feel.

McPhail brought Longarm's hotcakes, a tub of sweet butter, and a crock of sorghum syrup. "On the house this morning, Marshal."

"Hell, Harry, if I'd known I could eat here for free I'd've been taking all my meals here," Longarm said with a grin.

Later, that afternoon, Longarm let it be known on both sides of the street that he was tired and wanted to spend some time with a certain lady friend, that he would be unavailable until the following morning.

After that he disappeared from the paired towns. Liz at just about the time Longarm went into seclusion pulled her blinds and locked her front door.

The gray was left standing in the corral behind the smithy, there for anyone to see if they cared to look.

And there was no sign of their visiting lawman.

Chapter 58

Longarm shivered. He was sitting on the hilltop east of the lake. He had one of Liz's quilts wrapped around his shoulders and a .44-40 Winchester carbine laid across his lap.

He had dozed a little early in the evening but now forced himself to remain awake.

He was watching. Hoping the son of a bitch who set that fire would return and try to complete the job.

About three o'clock in the morning, judging by the wheel of the stars overhead, he heard something below.

Longarm smiled.

Someone was down there. He could not see well enough to tell who it was who had come a-calling, but there was a darker shadow among the dark shadows beneath the partially repaired water tank.

Whoever it was stayed low to the ground and kept going out from underneath the tank to the lakeshore and back again. Longarm could not tell what the son of a bitch was up to. Then it struck him. The guy was gathering fuel for his fire, pulling dried grass and piling it around the timber that supported the southeast corner of the water tower.

As silently as he could, Longarm racked a cartridge into the chamber of his Winchester.

And waited.

As soon as he saw the flare of a match he lined up the sights—convenient of the bastard to outline himself so handily—and lightly squeezed the trigger.

The Winchester bucked hard against his shoulder, and a huge blossom of fire momentarily destroyed his night vision, but down at the water tank he heard the dull thump of a falling body.

Without consciously thinking about it, Longarm quickly shifted position to the side so if someone took a shot at the muzzle flash from his carbine the shot would go wide.

There was no answering gunfire. He heard no one running away. And there were no more matches flaming.

Longarm waited a good half hour before he stood, his knee joints aching and his butt cold, and stiffly walked down to the water tower.

He reached into a pocket for a match of his own and tried to light it by scraping it against the heavy timber that was holding up the water tank, but the match would not strike.

He touched the wood and discovered it was greasy with coal oil or some similar liquid. Which explained the stink in the chill, night air.

He tried another match, this time striking it on the butt plate of his Winchester, and this time it caught fire.

Bending down, he held the match close to the body of the man he had just killed.

"Well, I'll be a son of a bitch," he muttered.

The firebug lay dead beside the water tower the man had tried to destroy, a flat-nosed .44-caliber slug square in his chest.

But why . . . ?

Longarm pondered the question for a spell, then pulled Liz's quilt tighter around his shoulders and started walking back to town.

Chapter 59

Word spread through Valmere like wildfire. Jacob Potts was dead, shot while trying to destroy the town's water system.

"What I still don't understand," Longarm said, "is why he done it. What did Jacob have to gain by getting rid of that water tank?"

"It isn't what he had to gain," Potts's brother Jason said. "It's what he had to lose. I hate to say this but . . . Jacob had a good thing here, and he didn't want to lose it."

"I don't understand, sorry," Longarm said. The other residents of Valmere crowded close to hear what the Nebraska Potts had to say, too.

"Jake didn't want these two towns cooperating on the water or anything else. You might have noticed that I serve a good beer and a superior whiskey. Jake cut every corner he could so he could squeeze as much profit out of his customers as was possible. When I sell a mug of beer I make two, two and a half cents profit on the deal. When Jake sold a beer . . . in an undersized mug, by the way . . . he planned on making at least four cents.

"Same thing with his whiskey. I'll make two or three cents a shot. Jake made his own nasty concoction and pulled in four to five cents profit per shot. He was greedy." Jason nodded toward the plump little black woman, who was standing on the edge of the crowd. "Just as Hettie."

"What does she have t' do with it?" Longarm asked.

"Jake was one of Hettie's partners in the whorehouse. I don't suppose he would have cared if anyone knew that, but their other partner was dead set on remaining anony . . . anony . . ."

"Anonymous," someone in the crowd provided.

"Thanks. Yeah, that. The other partner didn't want to be known, so Jake kept quiet, too. Hettie only owns a ten percent share in Stella's. Jake and the other fellow each had forty-five percent." Jason sighed. "Now I suppose I own Jake's share, me being his brother."

The crowd milled around in the dead man's saloon, everyone seeming to be speaking at once. Bartender George Griner could have used three sets of arms and six sets of hands to keep up with it all. Longarm suspected the place was taking in more money this evening than it ever had before. He even saw a large contingent of Stonecipher people who had come to listen and commiserate and drink.

Everyone else seemed to be wide-awake, but he was tired. He had gotten barely a wink of sleep during the evening and now was running out of steam.

He excused himself to no one in particular and walked outside into the cool of the night.

He turned to go back to the whorehouse and to bed but stopped short at the distinctive sound of a weapon being cocked.

"You son of a bitch. You couldn't leave well enough alone, could you? You had to come here and completely fuck everything up."

Without turning around, Longarm said, "Good evening t' you, too, Garrett. You're the other partner, ain't you? An' you don't want t' have to drop your prices to just a fair profit. You wanted t' go on cheating all the cowhands on this side o' the line. I'll bet it was you and Jacob working together to get the jealousy started and the lies about who was welcome where. Was it you that shot at me a couple times, too?"

"That was Jacob. The softhearted idiot. He deliberately missed. He said he wanted to frighten you away. I wouldn't have missed."

"No, I expect you wouldn't have," Longarm said, still with his back to Franz. "Do you mind if I turn around? I'd hate t' die with a bullet in my back. Better to take it face on an' proud."

"Go ahead," Garrett Franz said. "But slowly."

Longarm nodded. Slowly turned.

The big .45 already in his hand barked. Garrett Franz's mouth opened as if to scream but no sound emerged from his throat. Longarm's bullet ripped his throat out before the store-keeper could pull the trigger of the rifle he held in his hands.

Franz crumpled to the ground. Longarm walked over to him. Stood there looking down at the mortal remains of Valmere's mercantile owner.

"Huh," he said, shucking the empty brass out of his Colt and replacing it with a fresh cartridge. "Maybe you should've stuck to stocking shelves, mister."

He thought about the soft bed waiting for him upstairs in Stella's.

Then he thought about a different bed waiting for him across on the Nebraska side.

He walked on to Nebraska. And Elizabeth Kunsler.

Watch for

LONGARM AND THE YUMA PRISON

the 425th novel in the exciting LONGARM
series from Jove

Coming in April!